Spy Night & Other Memories
A Collection of Stories from Dick & Renée

By
Renée Richards

Keith Publications, LLC
www.keithpublications.com
©2014

Arizona
USA

To Art and Mary Voisin

Enjoy!

Renée Richards

Spy Night & Other Memories
A Collection of Stories from Dick & Renée

Copyright© 2014

By Renée Richards

Edited by Ray Dyson
Raydyson7@yahoo.com

Cover art by Elisa Elaine Luevanos
www.ladymaverick81.com

Cover art Keith Publications, LLC © 2014
www.keithpublications.com

ISBN: 978-1-62882-067-6

If you are interested in purchasing more works of this nature, please stop by
www.keithpublications.com

Contact information: info@keithpublications.com
Visit us at: www.keithpublications.com

Printed in The United States of America

Dedication

To Arleen

She could tell a few herself

Table of Contents

Introducing Renée

By Keith Olbermann, ESPN

Renée Richards has been to hundreds if not thousands of tennis tournaments in her life, and I've covered exactly *five* of them, yet it is because of one I went to that she *didn't* that caused us to meet, more than three decades ago.

I'm a very lucky guy.

Not that it seemed that way during the 1982 U.S. Open. After nearly two weeks sitting atop Louis Armstrong Stadium, the swaying of my head back and forth across the courts like a pendulum interrupted only by occasional squinting into tiny black and white television monitors, my head went from left to right but it felt my left eye had continued to look to the far left. I felt as if I had suddenly assumed a Marty Feldman-like, reverse-cross-eyed look. It hurt like hell.

I struggled to the office of my optometrist, who heard my story and then burst out laughing. "Who hurts their eyes *watching* tennis?" He finally calmed himself down long enough to begin a kind of weird catechism.

"I'm going to send you to see New York's leading muscle ophthalmologist," he said. "Do you know who that is?"

Holding my hand in front of my eyes to shield them from the glare of ordinary daylight, I answered "No, sorry, I must've let my knowledge of the muscle ophthalmology rankings slip."

"You did this at the U.S. Open?"

I started to nod then thought better of it. I grunted a "yes."

"I'm sending you to see Dr. Renée Richards, the transsexual tennis player."

I told him I didn't care to whom he was sending me, as long as they made it stop hurting. I think I mentioned something about going to

1

see a circus bear who smoked cigars if that was my option. He kept laughing while I kept swearing under my breath. "You'll like her. She just bought a practice from the estate of a pretty good muscle guy," he said. "She's not just the best, she's also really funny."

I got the appointment with surprising speed. I walked into a nice office waiting room on Park Avenue to find it empty, save for the receptionist, who was on the phone.

"No, I'd never do that, ma'am," she said into the receiver as she gestured me into a seat. "No, you can't talk to Dr. Williams (pause). No, he's not available (pause). No, I'm not keeping you from talking to him (pause). No, he's not refusing to talk to you (pause). No, he's not associated with the practice any longer (pause). No, literally, you *can't* talk to Dr. Williams (pause). Frankly, ma'am, he's deceased (pause). No, I wouldn't make something like that up (pause). No, he's not avoiding you (pause). No, he's really dead (pause). Well, I'm confident it was a great surprise to him, too."

Mind you, all this was *before* I met Renée Richards. These people find her. You will meet many of them in *Spy Night.* I sometimes wonder if they have been sent to her by an occasionally beneficent universe in the way it sent corrupt politicians to H.L. Mencken or entertaining baseball players to Vin Scully, because the two of them and Renée best knew how to use them as foils and contrasts, to give their lives meaning and pith.

Renée, of course, diagnosed what was really wrong with my eyes in something less than two minutes, even though the old head injury that was the cause was so off my radar screen that I had forgotten to put it in my medical history. I can remember her asking me whether I had hit my head in August or September two years earlier. She was testing her ability to put *the exact date* on the sequela she was seeing. When I told her it had been the last week of August she was delighted she had essentially split the difference.

"Your pain, we can cure for one dollar and 98 cents," she said, deadpan. "The root cause; that'll need brain surgery to fix. Not worth it. But here, take this pen light at arm's length, bring it to your nose, keep it in focus. You'll feel better by dinner time. Oh and you'll need to do this every month or so, forever. Your muscles are exhausted." Quickest, truest diagnosis I ever had—and the kind of unfailing expert precision I would come to expect from her over the years.

"Now," she said, swinging the wall-sized examining machine back into place. "On your questionnaire on which you left off 'I ran into a subway train' from your medical history, you write that you're a sports reporter for CNN. I don't have another appointment for half an hour. Let's talk about *that* for awhile."

As with lord knows how many other people—in that time and this one—Renée was the first transsexual I ever met and by dint of her extreme personal accessibility and her immediately evident skills and gifts, she normalized me. She fulfilled the unintentional education suggested by the data that would only be distilled a decade or more later (if you don't know somebody in a "group" your acceptance of that "group" is likely to be only about 10 percent; if you then *meet* somebody in that group it will jump to about 90 percent).

But more importantly for me, the remaining 28 minutes of my half hour appointment consisted of Renée asking me about whether I ever contemplated the impact of what I said on television, on the lives of people about whom I said it. She presented examples from her own very high profile life. I was dumbfounded by just how little I knew about the personal impact of media, but comforted that based on the hair-curling examples she gave that I didn't have far to go to ascend to the top of the list in terms of self-awareness. If my credo (it's your story but it's their *life)* wasn't born that day, at minimum, for the first time, it stood up on its own feet.

I'm very grateful to Renée. Besides which, she's not just the best at unintentional ethics coaching, she's also really funny.

It's probably two annual exams since my most recent ophthalmologist told me another story. He and Renée were two of the loudest voices at a contentious meeting about fees and privileges and rights at a prominent New York hospital. Sides were forming and the mood was growing ugly. As the anger rose, half the eye specialists—nearly all of them, men—were ready to capitulate and the other half seemed ready to fold. My doctor told me that just at the breaking point, Renée raised her voice and the room fell silent. "Gentlemen," she admonished them. "We have to act and we have to act *now*. We have to show them we have rights. We have to grow a pair."

The doctor said that when the laughter finally stopped, the leader of the capitulation group said, "Renée's right. We can't give in." In retelling the story my doctor laughed and marveled at the line and the timing. "But then, you know Renée. She's not just the best— she's also really funny."

As, if you don't know already, you will now find out.

By Mary Carillo,
former tennis player and sportscaster

So I'm a young tennis pro playing in the Avon Futures of Columbus, Ohio, in January 1978. Minding my own business, trying to use my flimsy forehand to win a couple of rounds and pay my expenses for the week. This was not a large tennis tournament, but if you wanted to make it to the Bigs you went through cities like Columbus. As it happened, two big stories emerged from this event: an unknown teenager from Lutherville, Maryland, named Pam Shriver came from the pre-qualifying rounds to win the whole damn tournament, and a transsexual named Renée Richards made worldwide headlines just for competing there. It was Pam who was the surprise, not Renée, who'd already been playing on the women's tour to some measure of success and a whole lot of attention. But in Columbus, Ohio, a few of her opponents took issue with Richards' medical history once more and walked off the court in protest. The father of one player explained his daughter's actions by saying that having to play against Renée Richards was "against his daughter's religious and moral convictions."

The player protest was making a lot of noise, so the Women's Tennis Association decided to hold a press conference at the tournament to defend and support Renée's right to play professional tennis. I had just been made a member of the Board of Directors of the WTA to represent the lower ranked players, and I was already in Ohio, so I was chosen to speak on behalf of the association. Well, sweet Jesus. Me? Really?

I arrived at the press center with an official statement and some notes to remind me to stay on message, and in a packed room I took center stage with Renée. Lord only knows what she thought of me in those moments, but I'm guessing it was, "Where's Billie Jean King when I really need her?" The media settled down and after I was introduced, I began. I looked at Renée and said,

"I don't know what the big deal is. I mean, just because she's Jewish."

Maybe I'd gone off the reservation a tad, but satisfied with my performance, I looked out at the gathered press people, then over at Renée again. She was wide-eyed and silent, until we both started to giggle. Then everyone else did too. The whole silly press conference was pretty much over after that. Renée said some smart things, and then she just kept playing. There were no more protests, and Pam Shriver became a famous tennis player that week.

And Renée Richards and I have been friends ever since.

I have heard some terrific stories from Renée over the years, and I've read her two books, *Second Serve* and *No Way, Renée*. I feel like a bit of an expert on her remarkable life and times, so I was delighted to know Renée had decided to sit down once again to document even more of her past. From the colorful childhood of Dickie Raskind, a nice Jewish boy from New York who comes upon a German spy at summer camp, to Renée Richards' final day as a famous, beloved eye surgeon, *Spy Night* gives us both lives in full- as a quiet, observant child, as athlete, celebrity, educator, dog owner, world class coach, and world class surgeon, too.

What a time she has had. I'm so glad she wrote it all down.

Foreword

Six Blind Men

The parable about the six blind men and the elephant seems appropriate for me to introduce a collection of stories I have written over a period of more than half a century. The poem by John Godfrey Saxe describes it well:

It was six men of Indostan
To learning much inclined,
Who went to see the Elephant
(Though all of them were blind),
That each by observation
Might satisfy his mind…
And so these men of Indostan
Disputed loud and long,
Each in his own opinion
Exceeding stiff and strong,
Though each was partly in the right,
And all were in the wrong!

In the latter part of the 20th century, I was perhaps the most notorious person in the world who had become a woman after growing up a boy and then a man. My fame came after my identity was disclosed when I played in an amateur tennis tournament in California where I had moved to start my "new" life, and then sued the tennis organizations, successfully, to be allowed to compete as a woman professional in the US Open Tennis championships in 1977. I became in an instant a pioneer for sexually disenfranchised people, at the time of the Cultural Revolution, the sexual revolution, and the battle for women's rights. After playing on the professional tour for five years, I coached all-time champion Martina Navratilova to several major championships and then returned to my main occupation of eye surgeon and physician, mainly for pediatric ophthalmology and eye muscle disorders. I wrote one textbook on eye muscle surgery, but I am better known for my two autobiographies, *Second Serve* and *No Way Renée*. In the present century I am hardly known in the public world at all, save for a few tennis fans who recognize and greet me at the US Open every summer.

The present collection of stories has nothing to do with my odyssey from man to woman, that subject is well covered in the autobiographies. In fact, the stories have nothing to do with sex, or gender, if you prefer. I wrote these stories to chronicle some of my life apart from what I was notorious for—interesting things I experienced unrelated to my infamy. And also to set straight some "opinion" like the *Six Blind Men and the Elephant*. One said the elephant was hard like a pipe because he had felt the tusk. Another said the elephant was like a rope because he had felt the tail. Each one describing what part of the elephant he had felt.

When I helped a man stricken by lightning at a tennis tournament in Jacksonville, Florida, he said to me, "I didn't know you were that kind of doctor." And when I was introduced to a new young colleague, a retina specialist in our New York City office, he said, "Oh, you play tennis. I didn't know that." It always surprises me when that happens, but not everyone knows "my story," nor the crazy things that happened to me unrelated, as one might say. Many sides to the elephant, for sure. These stories are all mixed together, some written as "Dick," some as "Renée," some from childhood, others in my dotage. Some are from my life as a young doctor in training and then a Naval medical officer, some as a parent, some experiences with famous people—all written in the first person—Dick, Renée, doc, "super senior," whatever I was at the time. Like Papillon, the famous Frenchman who wrote about escaping from Devil's Island twice, he did have another life of great adventure. So did I.

Spy Night and After

Remembering Deer Lake Camp

One

I knew we would miss the train; I knew it. My parents were always late for everything: social occasions, starting vacations, games, dinners, anything. Despite my frantic efforts to mobilize them and then my father's driving, careening over the metal slats of the Queensboro Bridge to Manhattan, and a frantic run through the train station at Grand Central, we missed the camp train, the train which was to take me and some eighty other boys off to summer camp at Deer Lake, near Madison on the Connecticut shore of the Long Island Sound. When I take the train to work even now from my home in upstate New York, walk peacefully past that four-sided clock above the information booth, and look up at the blue sky ceiling miles above with the constellations painted on it, the sun streaming in through the giant windows above the huge marble staircase at the east end of the terminal, sometimes I think back to the first time I was ever there, when we made that final dash to the track—"New Haven line to Boston"—with my train just pulling away.

My father steered the big Buick Roadmaster sedan out of Manhattan. All the doctors drove Buicks back then. "When better cars are built, Buick will build them," (so said the ads). I remember it was pouring rain. I sat between my mom and dad in the middle of the bench seat, my feet just touching the big housing for the driveshaft underneath, no sense insisting on sitting next to the window as usual. It was really coming down. I played with the radio, turning the knob as the little vertical line went back and forth over WJZ to WOR to WHN, and back and forth again. It was a two-and-a-half-hour trip, past the Bronx into Westchester County on US 1, and then into Connecticut, past all the shore towns—there was no Connecticut Turnpike back then, indeed not for decades more—past New Haven, where my dad would, as he did for years after, tell me about Yale University and how he went there and how I was to go there someday too, and at last arriving at Madison on the Connecticut shore. From there he turned inland four miles to an even tinier town, Killingworth, just a service station and a post office, found Duck Pond Road, then Paper Mill Road, and finally pulled onto the dirt road that ended in the middle of Deer Lake Camp, or Camp Deer Lake, take your choice.

Deer Lake Camp was not your typical summer camp with rows of cabins, ordered, laid out with purpose or design, like the rows of the army tents at Fort Dix, New Jersey, or the rows of cabins at Boy Scout camp. It was just there, at the end of and surrounding the dirt road. There was a main house, living quarters for the directors, Ralph and Elizabeth Hill, and the mess hall. I don't remember much else there because the rest of the place was out of bounds for the campers, except for a small addition that had recently been built, where the youngest group, the Cubbers, were housed. I was to be in the first group to stay there. Prior to that, the Cubbers lived in the "corn huskers crib," a tiny shack near the house. At the end of the dirt road into camp was a larger wood building, like the granges of farmers who had settled there in the 1800s, which served as the assembly hall on the first floor, and for bunks for two of the older groups on the second floor, the "west rancho" for eight-year-olds, the "east rancho" for nine-year-olds. Near that building was the shop, for woodworking, leather, and other crafts, the stable for the horses, and two other open areas. One led down to the lagoon, and, in the opposite direction, the other to the baseball field. Deer Lake Camp was not planned, drawn out, or designed; it was just there. In the middle of the area between all these building was the bell, up on a wooden frame, like the Liberty Bell in Philadelphia, only slightly smaller. It was a magnet for theft by the oldest boys who each year thought they were the first to have the inspiration of genius to steal it.

The lagoon was close by the main house and extended for about a quarter of a mile and fed into the larger body of water, Deer Lake, from which it was separated by a small foot bridge. Deer Lake, about a mile long, was the most beautiful body of water I had, indeed have, ever seen. No houses, no structures of any kind on its shores. The closest thing to such was the Pointers' cabin, the Point, where the oldest boys lived, at the end of a point in the lake about a half mile from the main camp. It was not visible from the lake, but close to the cabin was a small dock from which the Pointers could swim privately. The rest of the campers would swim at a tiny beach with a dock and an upended three-row bench which served as a diving board, around a bend from the Pointers' cabin. The only other structure anywhere near the lake was at the far end, some yards up from the shore and hidden from it, the lean-to.

The baseball field was rather rustic, homemade one might say, and the right field boundary quite short, good for us left-handed hitters, and the tennis courts were even more rustic, good for no one except Ralph, who thought it was a good challenge that grass grew right up to the baseline of the two dirt clay courts. The fence was not much more than some split rails holding chicken wire about three feet up from the ground. The corral was behind the stable, and if you walked into the "black forest" beyond the stable, you would encounter the campfire circle of wooden logs which served as benches, and then, well into the woods, the tree house. The only other structures were the cabins for the Loggers, the seven-year-olds, and the Woodsmen, who were ten or eleven.

We met the camp directors, Ralph and Elizabeth Goldsmith Hill, standing in the middle of the field near the bell, dressed in ponchos, Ralph without shoes or socks, Elizabeth with her full head of straw-colored hair in disarray from the wind and rain. They looked quite different from the first time I had met them, when they had come to our home in Sunnyside, Queens, New York, to tell my parents about Deer Lake. That was the only time I saw Ralph dressed in a business suit. At camp, when it wasn't pouring rain, I would come to know him always dressed in a sleeveless undershirt like a workman from Europe in the 1920s, like the men in Renoir's *Boathouse* often with a black snake wrapped around his shoulders, always barefoot. Ralph was the vice principal of the Walden School, a private day school in Manhattan, progressive in its teaching, politics and social attitudes. Progressive meant liberal, left-leaning, democrat, but not so far left as to be labeled pink, although that was to happen to some folks a few years later. He was about fifty, tall, rangy or raw-boned, one might say, slightly bald, with disheveled, graying hair. He looked and talked like a Yankee New Englander from down east Maine. But he was not. He was the son of Christian missionaries in Turkey in the 1920s and he had, without putting words in his mouth, none of the missionary zeal of his parents. I believe his religion was pacifist.

As I remember Elizabeth, she seems now a little like Golda Meir, the strong yet grandmotherly prime minister of Israel many years later. Golda Meir was robust like Elizabeth, but more stern. Elizabeth gave the impression of being much more like a gentle grandmother than Ralph was like a grandfather. Nowadays one might say they were a "good cop, bad cop" team. Although he meted out the punishments, she may have been the tougher of the two. She was the principal of the Walden School. Moreover, I knew nothing of her role in helping Ernst Paponak bring 200 refugee Jewish children out of Germany in the early thirties. How could I? I was only a toddler at that time, much too young to read *Out of the Fire*, his account of that endeavor. And that Elizabeth had a German mother and a Jewish father is also of interest concerning what happened years after at camp, as I will describe, but of no relevance whatsoever to that first meeting in the Sunnyside apartment.

They had come to our home early that spring to size me up, and to tell my parents about camp. Probably my parents found out about Deer Lake from a few of their friends in Sunnyside, parents of kids I knew. The camp was populated by boys from progressive, liberal, professional, left leaning, intellectual, first generation mostly Jewish-American families, some from Sunnyside, others from other metropolitan enclaves of similar background and persuasion.

At the end of the meeting I was to be signed up for camp. I also still remember my mother asking Ralph, "Why only boys at Deer Lake?"

His answer perplexed me: "Because girls are too tough."

I didn't understand the reason at the time, but I sure liked the dictate. No sister Josephine for an entire summer! And for all the summers to come. Free from her for two months a year was great. In truth I did love her; I adored her, and in actual fact she did get to come to Deer Lake once, a few years later. The year I was nine, a minicamp was held at Christmas time and there was a special dispensation: sisters were allowed. Of course she jumped at that chance, the chance to do anything boys were allowed, and girls were denied. In truth, I did enjoy having her there. We sledded down the hill from the main house to the lagoon. We skated on the lake, and fished for perch and sunnies through a hole in the ice. We cross country skied and tracked deer in the snow, and built big fires on which we roasted marshmallows and chestnuts and hot dogs. The only bad part of her being there was the play. At Christmas there was always a play, and my sister, at fourteen, being the oldest camper, winter variety, she was the director. It was a murder mystery and the butler was the murderer. Guess who she made play the part of the butler? Me! But I do digress. I couldn't help it. She really had nothing to do with Deer Lake, Spy Night, and certainly not the SS.

At camp Ralph and Elizabeth greeted us warmly. They were happy we had made the trip safely by car. I kissed my parents goodbye and thus began my career at Deer Lake. I did not know that I was the youngest boy ever to go to Deer Lake Camp, nor that I would be a camper there longer than anyone else in history by the time I was through. I was on my own, five years old, soon to be six. I was so excited. Why I was not terrified I do not know.

Two

My group was the first to be housed in the new addition to the main house. The new quarters even smelled of fresh-cut pinewood, with upper and lower bunks and a bathroom. I would learn that only the Cubbers were so lucky. Especially lucky for us because, only one year before, the Cubbers had to live in the corn huskers crib, the old shingled bungalow with the leaky roof and holes in the screens, near the stream that ran along the side of the main house. Even though I had arrived late I got an upper bunk. I even knew one kid, Eddie, who also came from Sunnyside, maybe his parents had told mine about Deer Lake. His family lived in Sunnyside Gardens, a model community of tiny two-story attached houses, surrounding a large courtyard, one of the first of the communities with shared property in existence at the time. (Still there almost four decades later, it enjoys historical status in New York City despite the fact the American head of the Communist Party was shot to death a block away.) It was nice to have one familiar face at camp.

I met my counselor, Lisa Stein. She was the only woman counselor in the camp, in fact, the only woman in camp besides Elizabeth. She stood out, not only for that but for the way she looked and the way she sounded. She was about thirty, with buck teeth and a full head of sandy hair in the tightest little curls I had ever seen, on top and all over, framing her face. And her accent, vaguely familiar to me from my grandma's tentative Yiddish-inflected English. It was guttural in the extreme. It was not exactly Yiddish; it was German, but not exactly German. She was ample bosomed, *zaftig*, as my parents would say. Lisa was gentle, but firm, a no nonsense leader of the Cubbers and a perfect bridge for the transition from the protection and indulgence of the families at home for spoiled five- and six-year-olds to the independence and responsibility of summer camp. I had no inkling then how different camp would become for me in only the very next summer.

Lisa was a refugee from Hitler, from the Holocaust, a word at that time of course with which I was not familiar. My knowledge of the atrocities was non-existent. The war was just then beginning. I didn't know it then, but I learned soon after that she had no one in America except for Ralph and Elizabeth, who had taken her in and helped her to get started here, and that she had escaped from something and was lucky to be alive. Where and how they had found her I did not know, but much to their credit she thrived under their protection. Years later they built an A-frame cottage for her in the woods, close by their own cottage just outside camp. I could understand Elizabeth befriending her but it seemed unusual to me for Ralph, Midwesterner, tough exterior; guess I didn't know him so well. As I look back I am proud of the way he safeguarded her.

She was a very good counselor for the littlest group. She could handle bright, rambunctious, spoiled little boys. I remember that first week of camp. I had never done anything for myself—nanny, maid, mother, and aunt all hovered over my every need at home. I had never taken care of my own clothes, and certainly never ever made a bed. The first night at camp I wet my bed. I had enuresis. Even at the advanced age of five I did it frequently, maybe a sign of some underlying unconscious problem. Whatever. I was required to strip the sheets from the bed, change them, wash the soiled ones and hang them up on the line outside to dry, all in full view of my old friend Eddie, and my new friend Jerry, who was to become my best friend at camp. I never wet my bed again, not that summer at camp, not at home after, never.

The Cubbers had responsibility only for things like their clothes and personal cleanliness, always brushing teeth or so it seemed. Fortunately a wet toothbrush was sufficient evidence. There was only one mandatory activity—afternoon swim, two actually—morning assembly also, but that wasn't exactly an activity. The beach, a tiny area of sand at the southern border of the lake where it emptied over the waterfall to the stream below, was where we lathered up with a bar of soap and jumped in. We always swam naked. There was a small wooden dock and three rungs of a wood bench ladder, the highest about eight feet up. I would dive off the lowest, but for the upper two I jumped. After the dive we would see who could swim the farthest underwater. Little Peter Buttonweiser, scion of one of the wealthiest German-Jewish families in New York, which had emigrated at the turn of the last century, could swim the farthest, so far in fact that sometimes we worried until we saw his little head pop up at the far end shore by the tree rope we used for swinging out into the lake and jumping off. He was one of the few chubby kids at camp, most of the rest of us painfully skinny. Maybe that's why he had a lung capacity far bigger than the rest of us. My best friend was Jerry Lambert, even skinnier than me. His real name was Jeremiah, but I was the only one privileged to know that. We did everything together, swimming, and hunting with our BB guns, canoeing, and horseback riding. We were so close we became blood brothers when we rubbed our arms together after scratching them bloody picking blackberries in the woods. His father owned a meter company and I remember after that first summer running down to our basement at home and seeing written on the electric meter there "Lambert Meter Co," my blood brother's company.

One of the most important freedoms of even that first year was dress. We could dress anyway we wanted. Tops were only required at meals, not even shoes. I usually wore blue jeans—dungarees—with my hunting knife in a leather scabbard attached to my belt, a Deer Lake T-shirt, sometimes a baseball hat. When the morning chill abated I would shed my jeans and shirt and wear only my skimpy, satiny, shiny latex swimming trunks. The license to wear whatever we pleased was a relief for me. My mother had strange ideas about clothing me. When I was four I was still wearing the long white stockings both my sister and I were put in, and even at five at home and at school I was still dressed in a starched, white, collared shirt with buttons that attached to my short pants. It felt awful to be dressed that way, all the other kids already in soft cotton T-shirts. After that first year at camp, my clothing emancipation was complete, or so I thought. I came home from camp all grown up.

The second summer at Deer Lake was a radical change. First of all, this time I made the camp train. And lucky for me I did. Turning seven that summer I had become hooked on baseball. My best friend at my new home in Forest Hills, Queens, was Robert Murphy, who lived around the block from our house. He introduced me to the game, the Yankees, and the major leagues. We would sit in his father's long-nosed Packard 12 cylinder sedan, drinking Pepsi, and listen to Mel Allen shout on the radio, "how about that, another Ballantine blast for the Yankee Clipper, Joe DiMaggio," after the Yankee superstar would deposit a home run into the stands. So I knew what our new counselor meant when he came to our seats on the train and told us a famous man was coming back to our car to talk to us. The manager of the Philadelphia Athletics, archrival of the Yankees in the American League, the regal Connie Mack, strode in and majestically stood at one end of the car. I thought it might be another one of the fantasies, or dreams I sometimes had, but no, this was real. The campers all huddled around him. I sat on the floor of the car in front of him and looked up at him speaking to us. It was like looking up at the Empire State Building, so tall a man I had never seen, like the cartoons of the exaggeratedly tall preacher in a magazine I once saw. He had on a coat and tie and a stiff, starched, collared shirt, and a black bowler hat. Looking down at us as from a mountain he talked to us about his ball club but mostly about how lucky we were to be going away to summer camp.

What a thrill. The famous Connie Mack—not only the manager of the Athletics, but the owner of the team as well—and the only manager to wear a coat and tie in the dugout, no uniform for him. After he spoke he went back to his own car, truly his own, for he had a private car which would soon disengage from the Boston Special and take him to his home in Meriden, Connecticut, for the July 4th weekend. Educated, rich, refined, stern, he was not like other managers I knew about: Miller Huggins, John McGraw, Rogers Hornsby. I can still see him standing so tall and imposing towering above me. I did indeed feel lucky to be back at camp, and more than Connie Mack would ever know.

Quite soon after we arrived in camp I realized my second summer would be a transformation. No bunk in an actual house, no woman for a counselor, and…responsibility. Each group had a job, always the same for that age campers. The seven-year-olds—I was six until August—were called the Loggers and lived in a small cabin next to the lagoon. Our job, as was always with the Loggers, was the pigs. It took a little getting used to the smell and the slop, but we learned to love them.

Our project for that summer was to build a fenced-in area for them that extended out into the lagoon so they could wash themselves and cavort at will. It was no mean feat to dig the holes in the bottom of the lagoon with a posthole digger for the vertical struts on which we attached the split rails for the fence to contain the pigs. It was a great satisfaction for us to finish it in one month. It also was our job to feed them, mostly garbage from the mess hall, and clean up after them. Woe be to any camper who shirked his responsibility. It was unthinkable. The times had surely changed from that first year of the Cubbers. Apart from the pigs, we were free to do whatever we wished. In fact, my friend Jerry and I decided we didn't want to live in the Loggers' cabin so we erected a tent close-by and lived there most of the summer.

Unfortunately we weren't the only kids to live in a tent by ourselves that summer, but the other kid was in a tent by order. Byron was a "deranged" boy; nowadays one would say "disturbed." In those days there were few diagnostic labels for his mental disturbance. He was deranged enough one day during a scuffle to sink his teeth into the skin of Jerry's chest and to bite down even harder, refusing to unclamp them when any of our group tried to get him to let go, Jerry screamed in agony with each clenching of teeth. Finally when he did let go, he was placed in a tent of his own. He had been banished from one cabin to another, regardless of age, until, the last stop when he had arrived at ours. He was about nine when we were seven. Turns out it was all my own mother's fault, which I didn't know at the time. My mother was a psychiatrist; and had encouraged Ralph and Elizabeth to take him as a camper. How could I ever forget that incident? I can still see Jerry lying on his cot on his back, Byron's teeth embedded into Jerry's chest. It had been a bad decision by everyone involved. And imagine that happening today, his treatment for egregious acts to be sent to each younger group, then finally to a tent solo, then out? And my mother? Only trying to do good, as usual.

The connection between responsibility and freedom, work rewarded by time and opportunity to do as one pleased, was learned early in my time at Deer Lake, and never verbalized. Only one job, and complete license to be free otherwise. I remember the next summer when our job was the chickens. The chicken coop was adjacent to the west rancho and it was our job to feed them. (Only at the end of the summer did we also have to chop off their heads, catch them after running about headless, and pluck the feathers out with them

19

upside down tied to a tree branch by the legs.) One time when it was his turn Chester Glatz forgot to feed the chickens. He was reprimanded. It happened a second time. He was reprimanded again. We told him, "Chester, you better feed the chickens." On the third day we all stood by, speechless, but some of us not surprised, Chester on the other side of the fence, in the chicken coop where he had been placed, without dinner, overnight. He never forgot to feed them again.

By the time we were nine we could take the horses out on the trails in the woods, but if we didn't feed them, care for them, no horseback riding. Same rules when it was our job to care for the sheep, or the goats. Responsibility and privilege. We learned about taking care of animals. We respected them. The black snake on Ralph's shoulders was a friend; so was Chip the raccoon who sometimes stayed in our cabin.

Apart from the one summer job, there were few rules. We didn't have to eat if we didn't want to. My parents sent up Bosco chocolate syrup to put in my milk. That was okay if I shared it with my table. And I would never eat creamed chipped beef, and oatmeal made me gag, so be it; it was my choice. We ate adequately but our ribs did stick out. We were skinny as rails, all except Peter Buttonweiser and Chester Glatz. Enough that we were so skinny by our own eating habits. Each summer, one day was designated when we were given only a little bread and cereal in the morning, then nothing. On that day, "care" packages of food, supposedly what we didn't eat, were made up and sent to Europe to feed starving victims of the war. The term "care package" was not yet invented, but that is what it was. "Austerity Day" it came to be called in later years.

By the summer I turned nine most of us had become sports nuts. We organized our own baseball teams as the camp had no organized sports. Dickie Brickner got us going. A first year camper that year, he looked around and said, "No baseball teams?" With the help of Bob Stollman, our aide—junior counselor really—we made up teams and played every day. We competed but winning was not everything. One day Steve Price got three hits off my pitching and I said, "Nice hitting today, Steve," as we walked off the field. (He reminded me of that on the golf course 60 years later. I had no memory of saying it myself. Maybe I got my killer instinct when I got older.) Eric Schwartz may have been the skinniest of all of us. One time Eric stepped on a beehive in the outfield and became covered with bee stings on his face and upper body. Ralph was called—there was no doctor or nurse. Ralph, not very sympathetic to the catastrophe, put mud on his face and said, "Feller"—he called everyone feller—"you will be okay; the bites will build character." I thought he was being cruel and insensitive, but maybe he was right. Eric grew up to design the Throggs Neck Bridge guarding the entrance to New York harbor. George Segal liked baseball too, but even more the mystery of the campfires at which Ralph would preside in full regalia as an Indian chief. George became a movie star.

Ralph set the tone for the camp, with his sleeveless undershirt and bare feet, calling everyone feller. He wasn't much into baseball, but he loved tennis, and he could beat anyone in camp. Even Mike Levinson, the only one of us who had had tennis lessons. Tennis lessons were almost unheard of then. Once when we had gone to town and I had won a rag doll prize at a country fair by knocking it off a shelf with a fast pitch, I brought it back to camp and it became the Raskind trophy for an impromptu tournament we arranged. I didn't even win the event; Peter Katz did. I was much better at baseball then and when I asked our counselor, Herb Steiner, if he thought I could make the major leagues some day, he answered, "Sure, why not." I was only ten. I never forgot his encouragement.

Baseball, horseback riding, trail rides, canoe trips on the Connecticut River, bike trips, staying overnight at American Youth Hostels, camping out in twos on our own in the woods, it was a heaven for kids from metropolitan New York. Jerry and I would stay overnight in the woods, with our BB guns, even a few times picking off frogs, which we broiled on a fire and whose legs we ate with gusto, catching perch and sunfish to eat, cooking bacon in a pan and then using the grease to cook an egg. Sometimes we used up all our matches before we could light a fire. Those nights weren't too much fun, but we still stayed overnight. Of all our wonderful activities the best was usually connected to the water: Standing under the waterfall, hiding out of sight from frantic counselors, swinging out on the rope from the tree branch, and landing in the lake, even the job of diving and picking the water lily roots out of the lagoon, helped by the occasional water snake or snapping turtle. I knew every inch of that lagoon.

The only times we were brought back into the real world, the world our parents had sheltered us from, was at the morning assembly. The assembly was on the first floor of what once must have been a local grange. Attendance was obligatory, like the afternoon swim. If you didn't show up for assembly, someone was dispatched to get you. Ralph would tell us about any special events for that day and sometimes tell us what was going on in the world. Of course there was no TV, no internet, no cell phones, and for us, no radio either. Sometimes he would tell us of world events. Hitler had already overrun Czechoslovakia and Poland, and was working on bombing Great Britain. Then we would sing some songs: "John Jacob Jingleheimer Schmidt, his name is my name too; whenever we go out, the people always shout, John Jacob Jingleheimer Schmidt." I remember that one. And "Down in the valley, the valley so low, hang your head over, see the wind blow." Sometimes "I've been workin' on the railroad." Even a few college songs: "Bulldog, Bulldog, Bow Wow! Wow!" the Yale fight song by Cole Porter. I knew that one before I ever came to camp. One of our favorites "Oh Joe Bernak, oh, Joe Bernak, how could you be so mean, to ever have invented the sausage meat machine?" Some of the songs I now realize had social-political meaning. "The sons of the prophets were hardy and bold, and quite unaccustomed to fear, but the bravest of all was a man I am told named Abdul Abulbul Ameer…and it went on to describe his arch enemy "Ivan Skavinsky Skavar." After the songs we would then go do whatever we wanted. Assembly, afternoon swim, show up for meals, and no one had to eat anything he didn't like. Heaven on the Connecticut shore.

Three

"The War" (no matter in how many since then our country has been involved, for my generation it will always be "The War") intruded to make us aware, even at camp. How could we forget those movies, like at the RKO Midway on Queens Boulevard in Forest Hills? At the movies there was always a Movietone newsreel and then a weekly episode of a serial, which let us know about the Japs and the Nazis and what they were doing to the Allies. The full-length movies, usually double features, would then depict someone like handsome Tyrone Power as the American Army captain in *Purple Heart*. The Nazis and the Japs were the villains. Even at camp and far removed from media the older campers certainly knew a little. Especially those of us with family in the war, and especially the Jewish kids. I had gone to Fort Dix in New Jersey in bitter winter to visit my uncle Albert, just 22 years old, where he was quartered in a big tent, wearing a long khaki overcoat, an Army cap, leather boots, with the other young men in his unit. He was about to be shipped overseas to England, Private Albert Raskind, U.S. Army Air Corp, (no separate Air Force back then.) He was in the 62nd Fighter Squadron, 56th battle group, 8th Air Force, and he was on the ground crew that would get the P-47 Thunderbolt fighter planes ready to destroy the Messerschmitt 109s and the Focke-Wulfs in dogfights over Hamburg and Berlin.

All that I knew very well, also that he had designed a bomb rack to make those P-47s into fighter-bombers. I knew even at seven that I would not see him again until the end of the war, if I were so lucky. I also knew Uncle Ben Raskind, gentle Uncle Ben, my father's oldest brother, almost too old in his 30s, was already trekking on foot through Europe in General George S. Patton's Third Army. Everyone knew about Patton's Third Army.

My uncles overseas, the movies on Saturday mornings, my parents conversations at dinner, the news they listened to on the radio, all had made me aware, and so did a few minor annoyances—air raid drills at school, with all the students herded into the center hallway, away from potential flying glass from shattered windows, air raid drills at home, too; a siren would sound in the neighborhood and then lights out, only a tiny bulb with a shade on top of it, stuck in an electric socket outlet near the floor for subdued light, and a man with a tin hat painted with a red cross on it, and a sign on his chest that said Air Raid Warden, walking about the block to make sure the lights were out. And rationing, gasoline and food. My parents were both doctors but only one "A" sticker, for doctors, per family. My mother's '36 Ford coupe had a "B" sticker, not as much gas allowed. And in the markets, only half a stick of butter per customer. One stick was a quarter of a pound. I would buy one half stick for my mother in one market and walk to another market and do it again. Shameful. Meat was rationed too.

At camp with each succeeding summer there was increasing awareness of the war. Even in summer Ralph was determined we should not forget what was happening. The day set aside for our food to be sent overseas—"Austerity Day"—continued and a few times during each summer we were also sent to a nearby farm to pick vegetables. Corn, tomatoes, cucumbers, all in a row, we tended to the plants and then picked them when ready to be sent overseas. At the end of the long row, there was a big bucket full of "belly wash"—like Kool-Aid of today—cherry or orange-flavored water, which we gulped in the hot sun from a big metal ladle. It was like the Victory Gardens at home but these were on real farms close to camp.

Another, much more dramatic event brought the war closer to us: "Spy Night." My first memory of Spy Night was toward the end of the season one summer when I was about eight or nine. We were told that four campers had defected. That word had not been invented as I remember, but that is essentially what we were told. I think Ralph might have said they were traitors or deserters, we understood that. They had left camp; they had become the enemy, and they would try to re-enter camp on Spy Night. The rest of the campers would form a ring around the main house, a line of sentries, to catch the infiltrators. Each sentry was posted about fifty feet from the next, and would march from one post to the next, and back and forth. The ring was about a hundred feet from the main house. If a spy got through the ring of sentries, he would dash to the house and the spies would have won. If none of the four spies got through then the campers won and Deer Lake Camp would have been saved, preserved from the enemy spies. The little kids took Spy Night very seriously, and even the older ones, who knew it was a war game, were willing participants. In fact, it was an honor to be chosen, or tapped, as a spy. It denoted a camper, like I would one day hopefully become, who had been at Deer Lake for years, a leader, capable, responsible, courageous, and of serious purpose. Passed over for selection a few summers, I wished even more fervently to one day be a spy.

The older campers took Spy Night seriously because they knew about real spies, and not so far away. German submarines—U-boats they were called—had been sighted off the New England coast, off Cape Cod, even in the Long Island Sound. And a few German spies had indeed come ashore and been caught. Their mission had been to destroy the harbor entrance to New York City at the mouth of the Sound, the harbor guarded by Fort Schyler on the Bronx side and Fort Totten on the Queens side. Of course skinny little Eric Schwartz, he of the face unrecognizable by bee stings, also thought of being a spy some day, not quite yet envisioning the Throggs Neck Bridge he would some day design bridging that harbor.

Other missions for German spies were to get on trains from Connecticut to New York City, to meet members of the Bund in Yorkville (the German underground in New York City) and to plan disruptions of the post office, the Grand Central Station, the New York Stock Exchange, and assorted other terrorist activities, with the promise of feasting after on wienerschnitzel and sauerbraten and downing lager from Munich at the Jager House on the ground level below Bund headquarters on 85th Street off Lexington Avenue. We were of course delighted when we heard a few of them had been caught.

One summer, I was nine or ten, or nine and ten, since my birthday was in August, when I was a sentry. I strained at my post through the whole night. Two hours was the designated time, dusk to dark, to see if I could catch sight of, or hear, a spy trying to infiltrate the line. When a spy did appear, not in my section, but in another area of the perimeter ring, I heard a lot of yelling, "There he is, running toward the house, get him, get him." And then he was tackled, caught. It was Gerald Freund, a "Pointer," from the oldest group. So it was a game, after all, but what if it were real? What if real spies were nearby? And Freund? Wasn't that a German name, German or German-Jewish? There were some doubts. And Josh didn't help. Josh, my dear friend (his real name was George, but more about that later) who later would go on to private school with me, and who was very savvy for a ten-year-old—he came from the Bronx— planted the seed of uncertainty in me. "Of course he was a real spy, know any other kids with a name like Freund?" he taunted. I didn't. And it was Josh also who informed me that Hammonasset State Park, with its beach close by the town of Madison, and previously one of our yearly trips every summer, only four miles from camp, had been officially closed that summer. The Coast Guard had set up towers at each end to watch the Long Island Sound for U-boats. "What do you think of that, Dickie boy?" he would remind me, more than a few times.

Spy Night only occurred once each summer, late in August. When I was ten my life at camp was quite full, and as with each succeeding year, more independence, more exploration of horizons beyond camp, either by horseback, or on the country roads by bike, usually with a friend, sometimes ending up at the gas station in Killingworth to buy sodas and candy. Often we would stop at the duck pond on the way to Madison, and watch the ducks and the turtles. Our group took a canoe trip down the Connecticut River, overnight, to where it emptied into the Long Island Sound near Lyme. I knew my father had had a summer job near there once at the Electric Boat Company on the coast in New London. I didn't know of course that twenty years later I would be doing training dives in the USS Sarda, the old World War Two training sub stationed at Naval Submarine Base New London in these very waters. Nor that I would one day take my turn on watch in the conning tower, long, long after there was any risk of German U-boats in sight.

We even went to the movies in Madison. Once each summer, we walked the four miles there and back to camp. One time we had to walk in pouring rain the whole way, and the theater was so cold we were shivering. Nonetheless, the trip was worth it, as I was enthralled by the young Estella, played by Jean Simmons, in *Great Expectations*, and terrified, when Abel Magwitch, the ugliest, most villainous person I ever saw, black patch over one eye, almost toothless, scraggly sparse hair on his scarred head, grabbed little Pip on the moors, after escaping the prison ship offshore. I was transfixed by Estella, and disappointed when another actress played her part as a grownup. When I read the book a few years later I only thought of Estella the first. George Segal was enthralled by the movie too. We laughed when he said he was going to be a movie star some day. I bet he didn't dream about Estella (the first) they way I did. I had some strange dreams in those days; sometimes I thought they were real.

I was eleven when I was in the Pointers, the oldest group. We lived in the Point, the cabin at some distance from camp proper, set back from the shore overlooking the lake. I would ride my bike back and forth to camp. I would swim off the Point dock whenever I pleased. I was a veteran, having outlasted most every camper from the age of five. Only a few of my friends remained from the early years. I spent more and more time by myself. I was also more sure of myself, so sure of myself in fact that when we put on a play in August and there was a part for a girl I volunteered. This was something I would not have done only the summer before. But I was a big shot, an athlete, well respected, not one to be trifled with, and there would be no ridicule, no questions asked, no eyebrows raised. I felt like doing it, so I did. I didn't even know why. Elizabeth provided a dress from her daughter Karen's closet. She said, "This will fit you, dearie." Nothing special about that, she called everyone dearie. I wore a kerchief over my short, short hair. And I put on lipstick. I don't remember the play or how the critics reviewed my performance. I do remember I never wiped the lipstick away; it just faded away about a week later.

It was toward the end of that summer our aide, Bob Stollman, took me aside one afternoon. "Dick, you are a spy, you will get your orders tomorrow." I had wished for summers to be tapped as a spy; it had never happened. It was like being tapped for a secret society at Yale, or for a U.S. Naval commander to become captain. I had thought I had been passed over permanently. I had wished to be a spy ever since my first exposure to that yearly event and now, finally, I was to be a spy. I had dreamed of exactly how I would do it too. I would swim down the length of the lake, enter the lagoon which bordered camp, and creep along the shore toward the main house. If a sentry came by I would submerge in the lagoon and breathe through a short rubber tube until he passed, then make my dash to the house. I knew I could do it. I ran to the shop and found a rubber hose. I cut it short, and I cut holes all over one end. I went to the lake and practiced submerging (long before the days of snorkeling). It worked. I mapped my route along the shore of the lagoon. I knew every inch of it. For years I had been pulling out water lily roots from its bottom. I knew I could do this. I told no one. I hardly slept that night. Did I know it was a game? Of course, but it was important; it was Deer Lake, and it was Spy Night.

The next day Herb Steiner, senior counselor, took me aside after assembly. "Dick, Spy Night is tonight. Disappear in the afternoon; your route is to come by way of the stream behind the main house. Good luck." Herb, who had given me such encouragement telling me a few summers before—"Sure, you can make the majors; why not?"—had now dealt me a death blow.

I was crushed; that route I knew to be a disaster. The stream was close to the house, the sentries were tightly packed there, and in the woods to the house it would be slow going, and the noise of my moving on foot would give me away. I tried, "Herb, I want to come on the other side, by the lagoon."

"No," he said, emphatically, "another spy has been assigned that route." I was devastated. I knew my way had a chance and that the assigned way did not. I understood I had to obey orders. North, south, east, west, four spies, each to come a different way, all four quarters of camper sentries to have some experience with a spy. If I came my way, there would be two there, and none by the stream. Just the same, why me by the stream, why me?

The campers were told at supper that four senior campers had become traitors and would trying to get back and take over the camp that night. A sentry ring would form at dusk and would patrol until dark. It was the campers' job to save the camp. If one of the spies made it through they won. I waited until well after dusk to start my stealthy path from the waterfall at the base of the lake along the stream that emptied below. The stream passed by the main house about a half mile along its course. I was good at this. I never wore shoes. I was silent, like an Indian. As a younger camper I had fantasized I was an Indian. As I got closer to the main house I could hear sentries talking to each other. I couldn't see them. I crept along the stream, silent, until I was close to the house, and waited. I tried to time one of the sentries' march by the sound of his footsteps. When the steps were farther away, I made my dash toward the house, through the brush.

"There is a spy down there, a spy down there," I heard someone shout. I started running and then I wasn't running anymore. I was pinned. Walter Marks had me by the legs. Josh was on top of me. "It's Dick. It's Raskind. We got him." Just like that. It was over. Not even a struggle, no punches thrown, no escape, no heroics, just pinned by Josh, who outweighed me by twenty pounds, and his helper Walter Marks, who had got to me first. It was over, just like that. None of the other spies got through either. Deer Lake had been saved another day. The spies had been crushed.

It was a devastating defeat and a lesson. It was not the only time I had ever done what I was told when I knew what was better for me, not the only time I did something I knew would not work. But it was one instance on which I would look back many times in years to come and remember the lesson of "wouda, shouda, if I only coulda." I had heard my father say that enough times when I was a child. And yes, I admit it sometimes did happen to me after that, sure, but not often. And then, I don't know exactly when, it never happened anymore—ever. Struggling with what I was told to do and what I knew was right for me to do. I had learned my lesson from Spy Night.

Four

I came back to camp for one final summer. I was a Pointer again, this time one of the oldest kids. I had been the youngest ever to go to Deer Lake, and now one of the oldest. Most of my closest friends were no longer there. I spent a lot of time by myself, paddling a canoe to the end of the lake, fishing for sunnies-or perch, sometimes a pickerel—you couldn't eat those spiny pickerel—and sitting at the lean-to up from the shore. I liked being alone. I had a lot to think about, a new school, what I would do with my life, as if I had any choice. Registered at Yale the day I was born, as the joke goes, "Sure, you can go to any medical school you want." That summer I was to have a special treat. I was allowed to stay for post camp after the regular season was over at the end of August. It was a privilege, a wonderful time, and came about by special circumstance. My parents were not at home. They had taken my sister on a two week vacation to the Grand Canyon as part of a group, on a twin engine D-C 3, a modern airplane at that time, almost the first fitted out for a charter resort travel flight. They couldn't come to pick me up. They wouldn't be home for another week after camp closed. Moreover, my Uncle Albert, who sometimes substituted for my parents on visitors' day, or fetched me at the end of camp, was still in London, otherwise engaged, with the 8th Air Force. The regular camp season was over on August 31st, campers having taken the train back to New York City, or having been picked up by their parents. This year, with no one at home to receive them, there was Dickie Brickner, Josh, and me, also Ginny Ginand and his counselor father, Carl. There were also a few other counselors, including our aide, Bob Stollman, and Lisa Stein. At post camp there were chores to be done, and the few campers there joined in to help load the canoes on the racks, close up the shop, get the horses ready for the trailers to take them to the farm, fasten the boards over the screens on the cabins, and get the goats, pigs and sheep ready for their winter habitat. Getting ready for camp to close was only part of the day. The rest of it was pure joy, only three kids left out of 80. And…whatever we wished to do, inside or outside camp.

Dickie Brickner was more intellectual than most of us, more thoughtful. Even when it came to baseball, he was the one who had first organized our teams years before, and he was a very good shortstop. He came from Manhattan. I think his parents were professors. He read books, and not just for school either. I knew Josh better than Dickie. Sometimes, I visited Josh at his home in the Bronx, a tiny house in a row near the campus uptown of New York University. He was as big as I was slight, large in all dimensions, body, legs, arms, hands, lips, even his large myopic eyes, with big thick glasses. We called them Coke bottle glasses. I remember playing stickball with him against other neighborhoods near his house in the Bronx. And we would listen to classical music on his phonograph machine that took up the entire space, except for the bed, in his little bedroom. He would say Rachmaninoff and I would have to say Serge, and I would say Puccini and he would have to say Giacomo. Rarely would one of us get stumped. I remember one: Mussorgsky. How was I to remember his first name was Modeste? Josh was ungainly in his movement and self-conscious about his physical appearance. Kind of an odd couple, we were very good friends. He defended me with his bulk, his overbearing. I defended him with my standing with our other friends: "Don't pick on him; he is a good guy." I would say. I forget why Dickie Brickner and Josh were at post camp, probably same reason as me—no one to pick them up. Ginny Ginand was there because his father Carl was one of the counselors.

On the fourth day of post camp I took a canoe and paddled to the end of the lake, where the lean-to was, and hiked up the path to it. It was often the place I went when I wanted to be alone. I was dressed as usual, blue jeans, hunting knife in its scabbard on my belt, T-shirt, baseball hat, no shoes. I wasn't really looking ahead, more down at the ground to see where to walk, and it wasn't until I got within twenty feet that I did look up. There it was, pointing right at me, the Luger. There is no mistaking a Luger, not for any 11-year-old kid brought up on the weekly serials at the RKO Midway. Nothing else looks like a Luger pistol, the housing sticking out behind the handle, the round cylinder perpendicular to the barrel which extended from the housing. And it is always in the hands of a German soldier, as it was now, who pointed it right at my head. The appearance of the proprietor of the Lugar seemed unimportant to me. All I could think about, fixate on, was the Luger. That the holder

31

was of average build, sandy hair, thin, young, and had blue eyes was immaterial. A Luger was pointed at my head.

In actuality as I would come to realize, he was not all that menacing; he even appeared frightened, but maybe that was because everything he said came out with an "etna" from the middle of his throat: "Are you, etna, Schtollman-etna?" The closest thing I had ever heard to that was from a little camper some years before who always covered his mouth with his hand when he spoke, and he too uttered a sound with every stammer of speech. Here was a German soldier, or sailor, with a Luger, and a sound came with his every spoken word. He wore mustard colored, thick cord corduroy pants, heavy leather boots up to his ankles, black turtleneck wool sweater, and a black wool sailor's hat. This was the end of August.

He looked me over, obviously relieved I was little and of no apparent threat. I was not exactly imposing, and hell, I couldn't even handle Walter Marks on Spy Night. His face was dirty. He motioned with the Luger for me to come closer and stand still. "Etna-ein?"—translation: "Just you alone?" (without the "etna")— and I just shook my head yes. He may have had a vocal tic, but I was speechless. There was a knapsack next to him, a canteen, and a hunting knife in a metal scabbard on the bench of the lean-to. I later realized it was a bayonet. After what seemed like a very long silence he said, "Schtollman?" with that same guttural Germanic accent that I had come to associate with my old ex-Cubber counselor, Lisa Stein. Exactly like hers, only with an "etna" in almost every utterance. I realized he meant Stollman, my aide, Bob Stollman. How could this German—sailor, soldier, spy—know Bob Stollman? I really didn't know what to make of that. He repeated it. "Schtollman?" He thought I was Bob Stollman? He knew of him? How could this be? This was a bad dream, only was it?

I had known about spies. I knew the stories of actual German spies who had been sighted, captured or escaped along the coast of New England and Long Island. Here was a spy. And he knew Bob Stollman, my aide, my favorite junior counselor, who hit all those home runs left-handed, like me, who was going off to college in the fall, Ivy League even. This spy knows him? They are in collusion? Unbelievable, and too much for my spoiled, protected little brain. I opened my mouth: "You know Bob Stollman?"

He said, "Gayenzi-etna-and kim mit-etna-Schtollman." Always that "SCH-tolman." Forget the "etna," there was no escaping that accent.

Bob Stollman was indeed at post camp. I had helped him take in the bases and some of the baseball equipment only the day before. "You want me to get Bob?"

He said "Jah," and "milcht and bread." I am sure he was as much surprised to see a little kid like me instead of his rendezvous as I was, so we were even there. Of course his Luger against my hunting knife tipped the standoff in his favor. "Ein?" he had blurted. Then "alone?" he had blurted. "Alone, etna" actually. First I thought he was just nervous; why shouldn't he be, but then the "etna" kept coming with anything he said. I knew about stammering. My Uncle Albert stammered, what a coincidence, but he was in London, his squadron dropping bombs right then and there all over Germany on guys who looked like this guy. How curious, the enemy stammered too.

I said, "Only me, only me," enough times to try to get the point across. And when he said, "Schtollman?" I realized it was not likely he had been dropped out of the sky, pin point onto Deer Lake, although that thought did cross my mind. He had a connection. Someone at camp knew about him, and holy cow, he knew about my junior counselor Bob Stollman. Could Bob be a spy? My favorite counselor, who hit all those home runs into the woods in right field, who was going off to college in the fall, who had risen to be a general in our yearly Spy Night event? Was he, Bob, in real life a real spy?

It was beyond belief, but then, here was a German spy with a Luger pointed at me, in the lean-to, and he stammers out, "Schtollman." He motioned me to come close. He took my hunting knife out of its scabbard on my belt. He frisked me, perfunctorily, thankfully, it seemed. Maybe I was trembling. I was certainly numb. He motioned with his stupid Lugar, over there, over here, directing me where to stand, and stay. Satisfied I was alone, little, and not threatening, he started asking questions. Who was at camp, did I know where Bob Stollman was, what was I doing there in the lean-to, and, did I know Lisa? Oh my God!

Of course I knew Lisa and I told him she had been my counselor when I was a child of five, which obviously I wasn't anymore, he should be aware. I mean, a kid about to go off to private prep school in the city, he should be aware of that. I don't think he knew much about prep schools or summer camps, or campers and counselors and things like that, even having been in the Hitler Youth Corps in Vienna when he was not much older than me. I don't even know how much English he really understood either. He knew it was a camp however, and he knew Bob and Lisa, but how I could not imagine. Most of what I knew of German soldiers was what I knew from those Saturday mornings at the movies. I certainly knew about their Lugers and the bayonets on the end of their rifles. I had heard from my parents too about German soldiers, Nazis they called them, and Hitler, and the Waffen SS (that elite unit-the schutzstaff—the protective force of the Nazi party) and the Luftwaffe, and Rommel's tanks and his Panzer divisions in North Africa. More important, I also knew from my parents something else: the Nazis hated Jews; they hated almost anyone who wasn't the same as themselves. And this young man looked just like a Nazi; it seemed to me, blue eyes, sandy hair, thick boots, and a Luger. And I dearly wished he wouldn't wave it around so much.

With not too much difficulty, he managed to convey to me that I would be as dead as a door nail—my expression, not his—with a bullethole in the center of my forehead, if I didn't keep my mouth shut, go get Bob Stollman, and return with him and food and milk. How he planned to kill me if I told Ralph and Elizabeth I had discovered a German spy in the lean-to I don't know. I just figured he would know how. If he didn't know how, then he certainly was putting a lot of faith in me, with his life in the balance. And he gave me back my knife. I still remember that. And then he waved the Luger once more and I was gone.

Five

I was numb, and my mind was racing as fast as I was paddling away from the shore. Could this be a dream? I admitted I did fantasize on occasion. I thought even I could have dreamed up this German soldier in the lean-to. But how could I dream up the "etna"? Maybe a vocal tic, maybe an "ic" or "ugh" or something like that. But not an "etna." How could I make up an "etna"—like the insurance company, The Aetna Life Insurance Company. I knew nothing of things like that. I couldn't have dreamed this up. This guy spoke with an "etna"—I never heard anything quite like that before The Luger and that voice, not just the "etna" but the sound. It was Lisa's sound, guttural, German, Jewish, and I did not even know of the word holocaust. That I was allowed, alive, to go back to camp, for any reason, seemed bizarre to me. Only five minutes before I was sure I was dead, at eleven, before my Bar Mitzvah, before my pitching debut at Yankee Stadium, before I would ever kiss Louise Wylin on the lips, before I would ever drive my own car. And yet here I was, hands tight around the paddle, paddling furiously away from my spy, closer to my friends and safety. Who could I tell what had just happened to me? What should I do? I felt suddenly responsible, now not just for me, but for my spy as well. I had never made an important decision before in my life, and now this. Maybe a little dramatic, but my life and maybe World War II in the balance too, what did I know? The most remarkable thing about it was that I felt responsible for my spy.

I sometimes wonder why I felt so impelled to do as my spy instructed me to do. At that time, I certainly didn't know anything about Jewish "guilt," being guilty for something I didn't do, or might just think about, or did do and shouldn't have done. Maybe I took it upon myself to safeguard him, keep him secret and out of the hands of the FBI or the Connecticut State Police, bring him food and milk, tell Bob or Lisa I had found him, because I was an obedient child and had been ordered to do it. Not likely. I wasn't that obedient. Maybe I did it because I remembered the movie *Great Expectations*, when little Pip came back to the moors with food for the escaped convict, Abel Magwitch, terrified though he might have been. Pip could have stayed home. He didn't, and I didn't either. Why? I certainly did not know my spy was one of the good guys, not one of the bad ones. Luger, German accent, giving me an order, certainly argued for bad guy to me. But he had not harmed me, he gave me back my knife, and he let me go. For whatever reasons, he trusted me.

That was it. After all he went through to arrive at the threshold of freedom, he trusted a little eleven-year old kid to bring him a little closer to freedom. And then there was his reference to Bob and Lisa. Especially Lisa. That he knew her was probably a very important reason for me to try to help him. I had not had much to do with her for the past six years since she had only been my counselor when I was five. But I did know something about her past I hadn't forgotten. She had escaped something terrible, and her voice sounded like my spy's, "etna" notwithstanding. I kept wondering had I dreamed this all up? I knew little of fantasies, or dreams, despite my mother being a psychiatrist. I wasn't a very intellectual kid. But I did have dreams, and daydreams, and some of them rather bizarre I will admit.

I stowed the canoe on the shore and walked up to the main house. Camp never looked so empty, only a few counselors outside, and more to the point, no Bob Stollman, and no Lisa. I don't know what I would have told them anyway, that I had a spy in the lean-to, that the spy asked for Bob, that he spoke with an "etna"? Who would believe that?

If I don't get Bob Stollman maybe my spy will kill me. If I get him, maybe he, Bob, will kill me. It was unfathomable that Bob, my role model at camp, could be a collaborator with the Germans. In point of fact, he was nowhere to be seen.

He had left camp that morning. Was he on his way to Brown University for freshmen orientation, or was he at that moment somewhere between camp and a rendezvous in the lean-to with my spy?

I needed help. Why I did not consult with Ralph or Elizabeth I am not sure I knew. Maybe I felt the spy was my problem, not theirs. And maybe I did have to protect him. Dickie Brickner was the first one I told. Thoughtful, measured, his blues eyes looking straight ahead under his blue baseball cap with the Yankees logo "NY" embroidered on the front ,he calmly agreed we had to find Bob, Nazi collaborator, heaven forbid, or not. And we couldn't allow ourselves to believe he was. But someone from camp had to know who was there in the lean-to, someone had led him there, and the spy had said, "Kim mit Schtollman." And then Dickie said, "We have to take care of this." "We," he said.

At supper we said little, which of course gave Josh the clue something was up, so we knew we had to include him. We told him, and then Dickie said, "Josh, you will have to swear you won't tell another soul about this. And where the hell is Bob?" Josh didn't know either. He said he thought he had left camp. We went to his bunk. It was cleaned out, no trunk, no clothes, nothing.

I was amazed at Josh's next declaration, "Don't be a schmuck; don't be a schmuck." It was his favorite line. "Tell him it's gonna cost him, hundred bucks for each of us. German spies have money. Tell him, for us to keep quiet, a hundred bucks each." Not "who is he?" Not "what does he want?" "who is his contact?" "how does he know Stollman?" "A hundred bucks each." That's what he said.

"Maybe this spy is going to kill us; maybe there are others hidden around the outside of camp," Josh went on. Dickie just shook his head. Josh continued, "Maybe he is escaping, maybe he is spying for the allies, maybe he wants to blow up New York. We have to find out. Maybe we have to help him, maybe we have to kill him." And then his ideas about our beloved aide Bob Stollman, that he must be a Nazi collaborator: "How else would this spy know him? And if we find Bob, all of us may end up dead. Let's get our rifles."

We did indeed have rifles, .22 caliber Winchesters, and bolt action, accurate at fifty feet for sure, even without a scope. And we had cloth patches from the NRA to prove our marksmanship. One of mine even had sharpshooter written on it. My mother had sewn it onto the leather bomber jacket Uncle Al had sent me earlier that year.

Josh was getting wound up. "We could sneak back to the lean-to and pick that spy off from the woods; he would never know what hit him."

"Don't be an idiot," Dickie said calmly. "He wants to be on our side; we have to find Bob." We never found Bob. And to tell Ralph what was going on we knew well would mean the Connecticut police and the Coast Guard would have the lean-to surrounded within the hour. We knew that. We couldn't tell Ralph.

What should have been the most fun of my whole summer had taken a strange and awful turn. The time I had sorely needed for my own, to paddle into the lake, the time I needed to think about my future, my dread of returning for another year to PS 144 in Queens, hopefully instead to go off to private school in the city—a huge leap—was taken from me. And the fear. So sheltered, the worst that had ever happened to me was getting beaten up by some teenage thugs in the bowling alley once on Yellowstone Boulevard, or getting taunted by the school bully in the playground in fourth grade. I had a nearly perfect existence up to then. And at home, I was the little *puritz*, the prince, always so spoiled. Now, there was fear, real fear, and just my luck, a German spy was my responsibility.

I was sharing it with Dickie and Josh, one who was cool and thoughtful, the other impetuous. There was only one other kid at camp, Ginny Ginand, counselor Carl Ginand's son—Ginny, pronounced as in "go," not as in "gin," and so called because of his last name, also with a hard G. He was smart and came from a different background than ours, a country boy, not a city boy. He knew the woods; he knew camping, even better than we did. Should we include him in our crisis? He wasn't street smart, but he was country smart, the kind of kid who could be on the top of the lean-to in minutes without the spy below knowing it. Ginny was different in another way too. He looked different at swim time: he wasn't Jewish. And he knew nothing about Germans. Maybe he should be on our team, but maybe he would tell his father. We would make him swear not to.

We found him in the stable, alone, getting saddles and bridles ready for the transfer to the horses' winter farm. "Ginny, we have to tell you something. You have to swear you won't tell your father. Okay, We have a German spy in the lean-to." First he thought I was kidding, it was so outrageous. He looked from me to Josh to Dickie and back to me. He knew we were for real. Not being a Jewish kid from the city, and as long as he didn't tell his father Carl, maybe, without prejudice, he would have an answer. Now we had four who were in on it.

The idea of shooting him from the woods, I am ashamed to admit, did have some appeal. "Do it and get it over with," according to Josh. "We will be heroes. He probably would never give us a hundred bucks anyway. What are they, German Deutsche Marks, Lira, what? My Winchester at fifty feet is deadly." All this from a Josh who was so myopic by age eleven he had to grope for his glasses in the mornings.

I said, "Josh, forget it. We are not shooting him. Ginny, what do you think?"

If Josh was Bronx street smart, city smart, Ginny was definitely Connecticut country smart. His dad Carl taught kids at boarding school in winter, and was camp counselor in summer. Ginny went along with him for both. He knew the woods, the horses, the other animals, maybe better than we, and mostly he was unspoiled, no Bosco chocolate syrup sent up for his milk, and I don't remember him with a three speed Raleigh English bike either. More important, his world was less complicated than mine had recently become, no prejudice from unfounded rumor, no negative opinion about any particular group of people, with no ethnicity, professional status, wealth, or other designations to stratify human beings or label them, or categorize them, or hate them. And he was fearless, not afraid of a dive from the third rung of the ladder, or of jumping on a horse, or of a coyote, a bear, or getting lost. More to the point, right now, also no fear of German spies, no knowledge even of Nazis killing Jews. Wide-eyed and wide-eared, he listened quietly, his face perfectly still, astonished at what Josh suggested.

And then he asked, "Why should we kill him? He didn't do anything to us, did he?"

Logical, fair, dispassionate, I was not surprised. Now he just had to help us decide what to do with the spy. A code name was decided, "SS." Not quite sure of its meaning then but it seemed right for our spy—the most sinister name we could imagine. Only years later would I understand how inappropriate a name it was for this particular spy.

Four smart kids, or maybe three smart kids and one dumb one, with the life of a young, stammering, stuttering, "etna"-ing German seaman on their hands. It seemed so preposterous, the only word I can think of, but he had trusted me, this spy, this Nazi, this Hitler, this deserter, this Waffen SS, whatever he was, from a German U-boat off the coast of Connecticut.

Six

Hitler was losing the war by 1944, but the German U-boats were still active off the northeast coast of the United States. Submarines had been sighted off the coast of Maine, Cape Cod and Long Island. The threat in Connecticut, in fact in Madison, only four miles from Deer Lake Camp, was so real that Hammonassett State Park, with its long expanse of beachfront on the shore, had been closed to the public.

All I knew that unfortunate morning was that my spy had blue eyes, he kept pointing a Luger at me, and he stammered, "Kim, etna, mit Scht-etna-tollman." What follows is my best reconstruction, piecing together what must have happened and what I later learned.

He came ashore, most likely the first day of September, in the early hours of the morning, not far from Hammonassett beach. Had he landed there he would have been picked up for sure. It was indeed closed to the public. The Coast Guard stations recently installed along the coast had brilliant beacons of revolving beams of light illuminating the shore of the Long Island Sound. Lucky for him, he landed a few miles north of the stations in a rubber boat. He and his partner made it ashore and scrambled beyond the beach to the uninhabited brush, beyond the dune. Their mission: to find their way to the railroad station and make it to New York City. They would rendezvous with the Bund, that is German patriots in Yorkville, and give them plans from Berlin for terrorist projects. SS cleverly convinced Klaus, his partner, that two would be more suspicious than one, and if one were caught, at least the other could carry out the missions. SS would stay overnight and find his way alone. He knew where he wanted to go, to the children's camp where his cousin was waiting. Had Klaus insisted on their staying together, SS would have had to kill him.

On foot alone he set out on the four-mile journey inland to Killingworth toward Deer Lake, compass in hand, and vague memory of directions in his head. To walk from Madison inland four miles would have been an easy task for a twenty-year-old seaman, but to do it alone, without knowing the roads, hiding a Luger in his belt, was not easy even in the early morning hours. God forbid he would have had to talk, stammering "etna" in his best Viennese German English. He crossed the coast highway, just two-lane US 1 in those days, and practically empty in the early morning near Madison. Heading north on country roads, only an occasional farmhouse to pass, he made his way past the duck pond, onto Duck Pond Road, then onto Paper Mill Road, and before daybreak he was at the entrance to Deer Lake Camp. He had made it, so far, with no need to kill anyone. I am not sure he would have been able to if pushed.

It was not so hard to imagine him covering the four miles over flat quiet country roads to the entrance to camp, but to find his way to the lean-to at the end of the lake, impressive. He must have had someone guiding him there, to be hidden and later to be transported elsewhere. He could never have made it to the end of the lake the way I did, by canoe, without being noticed. In fact he walked around the perimeter, on one of the paths the deer used to take, near the shore, guided by a German-speaking man who had met him at the entrance to camp. How they had coordinated his arrival, and how long Herb Steiner, my baseball counselor, one of the few familiar with the German language, had had to wait for him that night I never found out.

However he had managed it, it was just my luck to stumble upon him in the lean-to, the sanctuary I thought was mine alone. My plan, to rest and reflect on the next phase of my life, private school, new subjects, foreign languages, mathematics, things I knew I would be expected to become expert in, and athletics, baseball, football, tennis, swimming, all of which also I was assumed to excel in, all of that rudely interrupted by the successful arrival of that Luger to the lean-to.

Seven

Josh was nowhere to be seen, but to hell with him. Anyway we weren't going to shoot SS unless he fired first, and then we would probably be dead anyway, so what's the difference we realized. Dickie Brickner and I (Dickie Raskind) two nice little kids, still called Dickie not yet Richard or Dick, whose voices had not even changed, paddled quietly out of the lagoon, out under the footbridge separating the lagoon from the main lake, and then on up to the north end for our fateful meeting. We stowed the canoe on the shore, looking at each other for encouragement, for the courage to climb up the gentle path to the lean-to, to our rendezvous with the Luger, with SS. We heard nothing, we saw nothing, and when we got close, there was nothing. No Luger, no spy, just an empty lean-to. Dickie Brickner, he with blue eyes too, I had just realized, freckled face, thoughtful, quiet expression, just looked at me. Did he think I was crazy; did I make this story up? And if so, why? I looked at him, shocked, embarrassed, speechless. No spy, no Luger. I felt humiliated. We sat on the big log that formed the base of the open side of the lean-to, perplexed and scared. Maybe if he was indeed real, he was watching us from the woods. We took the food out of the knapsack; we made a show of it. We put everything on the picnic table next to the left wall and we waited. Nothing. If SS was watching us, he made no move to come forward. I even began to doubt myself. Had I been dreaming, worse, hallucinating. Was it possible there never was a spy?

We sat there a long time. It was getting to be dusk. Dickie Brickner, as expected, did not question my account, did not blame me for a lie. I may have had fantasies but I had never been one to make up stories to my friends. Our little dramatic interlude was simply a mystery, an incident, and he had the maturity and the sense to let it go. I was his friend, not a jerk. SS had split. So be it. But now what to do? Stay overnight in the lean-to? We did have provisions after all, and it wasn't cold. Or should we get the hell out of there in case SS decided to come back? We wouldn't be missed at camp if we stayed. The few kids at post camp were there on their own. We could have drowned for all Ralph and Elizabeth would know, or have been shot by a German spy in the lean-to.

43

We sat for more than an hour, paralyzed by the crisis, mostly silent. We didn't really hear the movement in the woods until it became louder, and footsteps in the rapidly darkening forest scared us to death. And then the shot, and another one, and a third. And finally out of the woods a figure came toward us. It was Josh.

"Jeezuz, you could have killed us," Dickie shouted.

There was Josh with his Winchester .22 rifle. "I just wanted him to think we had him surrounded," he exclaimed. Josh, whom we had not seen since late afternoon, had taken it upon himself to walk the mile and half around the shore on the deer path to the lake's end. He had arrived near the lean-to in time to spy on us sitting there, with no SS, and had waited to see if he would appear. What he would have done if he had, God only knows. Good old Josh, lucky SS, lucky Josh. When he became satisfied there was no spy in evidence, he gave me a tongue lashing: "You jerk. There is no spy. Dickie boy, you made it up; you are full of shit." I could say nothing. Why bother?

We built a fire and stayed overnight. Why not? Maybe the last camping out for the year. We had food, we were warm, and best of all, no one would be looking for us. If SS came back, at least there were three of us. I secretly hoped he would. He had disappointed me; he had let me down. He had not trusted me, and he had made a fool of me. "Fucking German spy. Who cares anyway?"

We awoke early, had some of the salami, and put out the smoldering coals of our fire. As we climbed over the big log, the floor of the open side of the lean-to, Dickie Brickner picked something up he spied on the ground. It had been lying against the outer side of the log, a small piece of cardboard paper, like the cover of a small package of matches, with some writing scribbled on it. Perplexed, he handed it to me. Then Josh took it to examine closely. So nearsighted he always did better with his glasses off, he held the printing right close to his eyes.

"What does it say?" I asked. For once he was at a loss for words.

"I don't know. I can't read it," he said.

Dickie got in the front of the canoe. Josh paddled from the stern. I sat in the middle and kept looking at the tiny piece of paper, some pencil lines, and a few words, undecipherable, scattered near them.

We docked the canoe. We had our story rehearsed: we just decided to spend one more overnight at the lean-to before going home to our parents and back to school. We ran up the hill from the lagoon.

"Let's play baseball," Dickie said. "One more game, the last one." And we did. And it was, without our junior counselor, Bob Stollman, without watching him hit another monster shot into the right field woods. He was nowhere to be seen. Maybe he was helping stow the tools in the shop, or helping with the horses. Who cared?

The next day was our last at post camp, and although I did not know it then, my last day ever at Deer Lake Camp. Almost everything had been attended to, the animals, the gear, the cabins secured with wood flaps over the screen doors and windows. Only Ralph and Elizabeth and a few counselors were there to bid us goodbye. It did seem unusual, too, no Lisa. She was always close to Ralph and Elizabeth. No Lisa, no Bob Stollman. Ginny Ginand's father Carl drove Dickie and Josh and me to the train station in Madison for the trip to New York. Carl knew nothing of our adventure. Ginny had kept still.

On the train we swore to keep our experience a secret. Even Josh. And even after he had once more scrutinized that little scribbled paper, he teased me one final time: "Well, Dickie boy, there was no spy, you jerk." He knew better; we all did. Maybe no spy, but no Deer Laker wrote that scribble. He knew it. We all knew it.

Many years later I found out Lisa Stein, my first counselor, was my spy's cousin. If he, here called SS because I didn't know his name then, could only get off his sub anywhere within miles of Hammonassett, she would figure out the rest. Lisa and SS, related, but not closely, had been brought up not far from each other in Vienna. SS's mother was Catholic. I don't know how much Jewish he was, but he was in the Hitler Youth Corps. Lisa had taken a different path. In spite of the obstacles put in the way of Jews to

45

come to the United States at the beginning of the war, Lisa had made her way to New York City, a refugee from Hitler, alone, aided by Elizabeth Goldsmith Hill. She was a teacher who wanted to study psychology.

It was rare but not unheard of, that one could be enrolled in the Hitler Youth Corps and not be true full blood Aryan. SS had one Jewish grandfather. He was a *mischling*, (slang for cross-breed), not likely to be a high officer of the Reich, certainly not likely in the Luftwaffe, nor in Rommel's tank corps. Lucky for him it was only one Jewish grandfather. He was a second degree *mischling*. Had he had two Jewish grandparents and thus be a first degree *mischling*, it was doubtful he could have structured his life to come ashore that night off Hammonasset State Park in 1944. No *mischling* of any degree could ever ascend to the Waffen SS. He had joined the army out of high school, his future as a medical student guarded, not optimistic in 1942. How he found his way to the submarine corps and how he was picked to be one of the spies to land in America is testimony to his genius, and his will to pursue his life. And how he kept in touch with his cousin Lisa in America is even more astounding, but somehow he did. Writing letters would be impossible, with censorship on both sides. Short wave radio was a possibility but also very difficult for both. Maybe they used Morse code, and more likely, maybe couriers, go-betweens. Who would Lisa Stein know, who could contact a spy on a German sub, and how would SS let Lisa know when and if he were coming ashore? Maybe the time and place were never set.

Eight

My mother was actually there at Grand Central Station when the train pulled in, on time, my father waiting in the Buick out on Lexington Avenue. She saw I was "in one piece." as she would say, and seemed no worse for wear, maybe an inch longer, although I was still a peewee compared to some of my friends. And when she asked about post camp, I said, "It was Okay." My father drove us home to Forest Hills. I was happy to see my big Airedale terrier, Clipper, even happy to see my sister Josephine. I even thought someday of telling her what happened at camp, yeh, maybe someday. I never did. I never told anyone. My mother found the piece of matchbox paper with the scribbled message on it in my blue jeans pocket. I saw her look at it. She had no idea what it was. She had studied German in college, but she gave no hint the scribble meant anything. She threw it away.

It had been indeed my last summer at Deer Lake Camp. I was going off to my new school in the Riverdale section of the Bronx, four changes on the subway, almost two hours each way, to the Horace Mann School for Boys high on the top of the hill, beyond the last stop of the subway, an elevated train by the time it reached Riverdale. Its gray stone schoolhouse with gothic casement windows loomed high and foreboding as we climbed the hill to the campus. Josh was there too. Yes, we did call our teachers Sir, we did wear coats and ties to class, and the headmaster was Dr. Charles C. Tillinghast and a Dr. Tillinghast is indeed what he looked like, no nonsense, headmaster he was—white hair, wire framed glasses, distinguished, imposing.

I would also start to spend the first of many summers at Camp Moosilauke, run by Moose Miller, the athletic director at Horace Mann. It was a much more traditional camp, with organized sports, a lot of baseball, and even softball after dinner with the counselors playing with us. Right up my alley by then; I was almost grown up. I remember well the first summer there, in August, when our counselor got a few of us together one day and announced President Harry Truman had declared on the radio that the war against Japan was over. V-J Day it was called (Victory over Japan). Our counselor said a U.S. Navy bomber, a twin engine B-25 named the Enola Gay had dropped a bomb-called an atomic bomb—with the explosive force of more than 20,000 tons of TNT on Hiroshima, a Japanese city, and then a few days later another one on Nagasaki, forcing the Japanese to surrender. The war was over on both fronts, and my Uncle Albert and my Uncle Ben would be coming home from overseas. Back at Deer Lake Camp, Ralph would build a big bonfire and all the campers there would sing songs in celebration. And there would never be another Spy Night.

Ralph and Elizabeth kept Deer Lake going a few years more, past the end of the war, into the '50's, years of the mounting Russian threat, the House Committee on Un-American Activities, and the Cold War with the Soviets. Although they were the principal and vice principal of the Walden School, progressive and liberal, yes, maybe even "pink," they were, as far as I ever knew, uninvolved politically. In 1959 the camp was closed. A camper had died from contracting tetanus; it would have been difficult to carry on. Ralph and Elizabeth lived in a small log home they built just outside camp. And Lisa Stein lived part-time in the A-frame wood house they had built for her near their own just outside camp. During the academic year, she practiced as a clinical psychologist in New York City. She never lost her guttural accent, nor her tightly wound curls on her full head of hair. Had she ever met up with her cousin SS, had she managed to guide him, conceal him, get him to the FBI? I never found out. I had occasion to call her once, maybe thirty years after my Deer Lake summers. I couldn't get out any questions about SS. I just couldn't bring myself to ask her. Instead I asked her what she had thought of me as a little boy at camp. I was into self-awareness, self-examination at that time, and I was hoping she could give me some insights from having been my counselor when I was five. She didn't reveal much, "just an ordinary little boy," or so she seemed to suggest.

And Bob Stollman? A traitor? A hero? Had he managed to find SS and usher him out of camp secretly? He had been a smart young man—he went to Brown University after that final Deer Lake summer and then on to the Harvard Business School. I guess he would have been smart enough to lead a spy on our side to safety. But why? Bob Stollman is still alive, now into the 21st century and I tracked him down not long ago. I wanted some answers to these questions. What did I learn? First, he said he was 81 years old and still lived near Teaneck, New Jersey. Second, he indeed did remember me at camp almost 70 years ago—"skinny little kid, lefthanded like me, always playing ball," he said. He didn't even do a double take when I said, out of the blue, these decades later, "Hi, this is Renée Richards." So what did I learn from him? This is what I learned: he had hit 107 home runs into the woods beyond right field at Deer Lake Camp. And he didn't even specify "single season" or "cumulative." I swear that's all he said. That was it.

Nine

I remember a luncheon once at the home of my professor, Dr. Herman Burian, in Iowa City in 1966. I was a post-graduate fellow in ophthalmology there, having just completed my active duty tour as a medical officer in the U.S. Navy (and yes, I had participated in some submarine cruises myself off the Connecticut shore only a year before, any connection between those cruises and my memories of another submarine event many years before had eluded me for years until that luncheon, when I abruptly was forced to think back to my days at Deer lake Camp and Spy Night and SS in the lean-to with his Luger.)

I had earned a prestigious fellowship, called the Heed Foundation fellowship, and the directors of the foundation had kept the fellowship reserved until my tour of active duty was over. In fact the fellowship director had tracked me down during my final year of active duty to tell me of this. I was in Iowa City to study with one of the best in my specialty field—ocular motility and binocular vision (children and adults with eyes that don't work together). At that time, several departments at the University of Iowa medical school were magnets for young specialists from all over the world seeking advanced training. The luncheon at Dr. Burian's was in honor of a professor, a woman, who had come from Tubingen medical school in Germany to give a lecture on a new type of visual field testing, three dimensional, but not computerized like now. Many of those invited to the luncheon originally were from Europe, faculty and students as well, and without making a conscious decision to do so, after about a half hour, everyone at the table was conversing in German.

All, that is, except me. I didn't understand a word, but I did have a remarkable learning experience while listening. One of the guests, a tall man with short, cropped gray hair, and piercing blue eyes was expounding on his experience with visual field testing in patients with seizure disorders. I heard him expound: "and the parieto, 'etna' temporal lobe 'etna' pathology 'etna' can be correlated…"

I don't remember the end of his sentence. I just looked over at him, in shock, momentarily frozen in another time and place, and then remembering, almost instantaneously, remembering from long ago that face and mostly that voice.

I was brought back to the present quite suddenly, when Professor Fred Blodi, the head of the department, looked at me, smiled, and exclaimed, "What is this with you, Dick, you have a congenital anomaly? You are not speaking German?" He knew of course I didn't know the language. He stopped everyone at the table: "Enough, enough. One of our fellows" (post graduate fellows) "does not speak German, so English, please, English."

Of course they complied, embarrassed at their rudeness for lapsing into their mother language and leaving one young graduate student out of the conversation. It really had not mattered. I understood something more important, to me, than professor Blodi could ever imagine. And now I even knew his name, Rainer. Funny kind of name. First name? Last name? It wasn't important.

The luncheon was over. I walked out with a friend from the eye department, Otto Weil. "Some crowd, Otto," I said. "Only in Iowa City, only in Iowa City." He knew what I meant, an all German luncheon, or almost. Dr. Burian was from Yugoslavia; Dr. Blodi from Austria, likewise one of the other guests, Rainer, who had maybe lost a little of his German accent, but assuredly not his "etna."

Otto had on occasion come with me to the tiny local airport outside town, where I had been taking flying lessons. He sometimes came along for a ride in my Piper Cherokee 180. He still liked to fly, even long after his days in the Luftwaffe in the cockpit of his Messerschmitt 109. It was curious to me that he never liked looking at the vintage P-51 Mustang parked in front of the airport. It made him very uneasy, almost perspiring at its sight. He told me why. His Messerschmitt 109 had been no match for the Mustang in the skies over Germany during the war. And he once told me why he was in the 109 instead of one of the elite Focke-Wulfs that *were* indeed a match for the Mustang. He was a mischling. Somewhere way back in his family, there was Jewish blood. So he was not likely to become a high officer in Hitler's Luftwaffe, just a lower ranked pilot, sent up in a 109 to get lost over the Baltic Sea and to find his way home on his own. There were no super navigation systems in the 109s.

Otto and I were good friends in Iowa, but I never saw him again after that fellowship year. He went off to somewhere in Wisconsin to practice ophthalmology and I returned to New York, in the airplane in which I had learned to fly, to assume my new job as resident instructor in ophthalmology at the Manhattan Eye and Ear Hospital. But before that fellowship year was over I did learn something from him I had wondered about for many years. One day not long after the luncheon for the German woman who demonstrated her visual field technique, Otto mentioned the guest who startled me back to my childhood, the one with the "etna."

"You know, Dick, the one with the stammer?"

"Yes," I said, "I remember."

"You know, he is a mischling, like me. He managed to come here during the war. He had relatives here. He had almost no opportunities in Germany or in Vienna. We had a nice chat, he and I, two mischlings."

Rainer was even in the tank corps, a lowly private. Otto told me once about Rainer being sent to a farmhouse near Budapest to get food, and while he was gone an American tank came around the bend and his tank had to disappear fast. When Rainer came back with the food from the farm—no tank. He was shocked and terrified, a suspicious guy to begin with I would say. I can only imagine the scene. Well, his tank came back for him early the next morning. I was a bit confused so I said, "Otto, you sure he was in Rommel's tank corps? No where else?"

He chuckled, "Oh, yes, he doesn't talk about it much but he was on a U-boat once too. He did admit that."

I did not comment on his brief history of Rainer's military career. I only ventured, "Otto, that is very interesting, I mean, about the mischlings and the war. It must have been quite a time." I thought to myself I wished I knew his name was Rainer, and we had called him SS. We had given our mischling a name that didn't fit. A mischling might achieve a position as a middling officer in the Luftwaffe, even in Rommel's Panzer tank division, but never ever could a mischling ascend to the Waffen SS. We had given our spy an impossible name.

Ten

The memories of Deer Lake Camp never faded for me, nor did they for some of my friends who were campers there with me. However, I never did learn how the camp came into being, nor about the principles on which it had been designed, even after a visit from Pete Hill, Ralph's son, who had been my counselor one summer. Pete, age 85, came with his wife, Marty. They live in a communal group in Ohio. We enjoyed talking about camp days, but he said little I didn't already know, except Ralph was not a Yankee from downeast Maine, as I had always thought, but was instead a Midwesterner from Kansas, the son of Christian missionaries in Turkey in the 1920's. I found out too that Ralph had none of the missionary zeal of his parents, and was a pacifist besides. My image of him with his sleeveless undershirt, black snake rapped around his shoulders, meting out punishments for failure to feed the chickens or worse, did not seem to fit. But the knowledge of how he had safeguarded Lisa Stein did.

A small group of us went back for a private reunion to Deer Lake, some twenty-five years after we had been campers. It was in the fall. Deer Lake had become a Boy Scout camp by then. A troop from New Britain, Connecticut, owned it. There was no one around when we explored some of our old haunts, the treehouse in the black forest, the Pointers' cabin set back from the shore of the lake, and we trekked through the woods to stay overnight in the lean-to at the end of the lake. Peter Katz was designated firemaster, and he reminded me it was he who had won the Raskind trophy in tennis long before I had become a competitive tennis player. He had gone into the world of theater and had become a producer of Broadway plays. Walter Marks, gentle, kind, artistic, had become a writer of music, and even of some Broadway musicals. I doubt he even remembered pinning me to the ground when he saw me coming through the sentry line as a spy one night so long ago. We talked about Jerry Lambert, who always said he would someday go to college "at Harvard, Yale and Princeton." We laughed, but he did. We never heard from him after Deer Lake, blood brother he and I had been notwithstanding. We mentioned Bob Stollman, our aide, but there was nothing said about that day at camp when I had found my spy. Walter and Peter knew none of that. Only about how

Bob had been a role model for us at camp. Lisa Stein was not mentioned. She was a counselor for me as a five-year old, not for Peter and Walter, who had come to camp a few years later.

We stayed overnight, cooked a dinner of hamburgers and hot dogs, drank a few beers, and I fell asleep on that straw dirt floor, thinking back to my spy, and Josh and Dickie Brickner. Dickie went to a small liberal arts college in New England. He became a paraplegic when he put his foot on the clutch of a British MG convertible instead of the brake. He didn't know how to drive a stick shift car. He also became a professor of English and creative writing and wrote novels. Josh went to Columbia University and NYU medical school, and trained in ophthalmology at the Manhattan Eye and Ear. He kept guns, even as an adult, and one time he shot a would-be thief from his fifth floor walkup apartment on 52nd Street on the eastside of Manhattan. The surprised thief had tripped the alarm on Josh's Corvette convertible parked below. He left a trail of blood as he stumbled to the subway on Third Avenue. Maybe Josh had him confused with a spy. Josh was an inveterate New Yorker; he practiced on Park Avenue for many years. Always willing to try something new, he was the first ophthalmologist to bring soft contact lenses to America. He bought a farm in Connecticut in his later life, retired, and played with his backhoe and other tools of country living until he died in his fifties there of cancer, having smoked cartons of unfiltered Camel cigarettes and having drunk six pack after six pack of Ballantine Ale daily his entire adult life.

Most of the others of our crowd at Deer Lake went on to interesting careers. None of them had participated in the well-being or otherwise of our spy. Each of them, I am sure, would have reacted differently from Josh, or Dickie, or Ginny Ginand, or me. Unfortunately for them, they never had that opportunity.

Afterword

July 1, 2011
Karen Hill
Lexington, Massachusetts

Dear Karen,

I tracked you down through my brother-in-law Peter von Hippel, who went to Cambridge Latin School with your brother, Mickey. I asked him for Mickey's address because I am working on a story and something of a history of Deer Lake Camp. He learned that Mickey is no longer alive and he got your address for me. I hope you don't mind my contacting you. I have been unable to learn much on the internet about the old Deer Lake. I am interested in your parents, Elizabeth and Ralph, how they came to start Deer Lake, and anything about the counselors and campers who were there. I remember Lisa Stein, my counselor in the Cubbers, Bob Stollman, our aide, Herb Steiner, Carl Ginand, and of course your brother Pete, who was one of my counselors.

You might not remember, but I met you once or twice. We are about the same age. Once for sure during Christmas vacation when there was a mini-camp and even girls were allowed. My sister Jo was there. My name in those days was Dick Raskind. I started at Deer Lake at age five and stayed until I was twelve. My experience at camp there was a very important part of my education and my development.

I hope you can direct me to some literature or contacts that might help me in this research. With best wishes,

Sincerely,
Renée Richards

P.S. The snapshot, circa 1943, is of your mother and mine watching me play ping pong.

January 25th, 2014 e-mail from Karen Hill Safford:

Hi, Renée,

It was fun for me to go back to Deer Lake. That was quite a tale. Is the SS [Rainer] part really true or added for flavor?

Liz was a co-director of Walden and Ralph was a teacher. He had directed another camp before my time in Massachusetts. When Liz inherited some money they thought it was a wonderful opportunity, especially for Ralph, to buy a property in the country and create a camp.

Lisa was sort of a second mother to me. She would be so pleased with your description of her as a counselor. I remember her telling me that you called her many years later to ask what she remembered about you.

By the way, she was a teacher and a Child Care Center director. Liz was the psychologist. Also, Ralph's parents weren't missionaries. Ralph was a missionary in Turkey for two years. He was there with his first wife, Pete and Barb's mother. They just got back, perhaps the last boat before WWI made travel difficult.

I don't remember meeting you or your sister. I do remember hearing about you: an all around good camper, a good sport, gets along with both kids and adults, great tennis player, participates in lots of activities, a happy kid, etc. Thanks for sharing the Deer Lake story with me, Karen.

He Came to Manhattan from 'Down Maine'

It was the first week of my residency training in ophthalmology at the exalted Manhattan Eye, Ear and Throat Hospital. The six of us—the first-year residents—were put to work staffing the clinics, with the surgeon director, whose clinic bore his name—Paton clinic on Monday, Troutman clinic on Tuesday and so on, coming and going to supervise the care of the patients "on the bench," the long clinic bench with the one desk at the end where the head resident, or sometimes the director, would make final decisions about treatment. The East Eye Clinic on the east side of the hospital facing toward Second Avenue consisted of four long benches with one desk at the very end. A spacious room, well lit by large windows for daylight, the desk at one end was where patients' histories were taken, prescriptions given. The actual examination was done in the adjoining room, dark, where three slit lamp biomicroscopes were situated and the resident would look at the patients' eyes—the patient sitting with his or her chin on the chin rest, the resident sitting opposite on the other side of the little table under the microscope, peering thru the binocular scopes at cataracts, corneal opacities, and any other pathology in the front section of the eyes.

Since we were thrown right into the clinic, no actual orientation, we were grateful there was usually a second-year resident in the room whose advice we could seek, besides the one attending surgeon who marched here and there. More important to this story, not only were we uninitiated novices in the care of eye disorders, we hardly knew each other—perfunctory introductions the day we arrived, that was it. "Hi, Dick Raskind here, New Yorker, from Lenox Hill (where I interned) or "Hi, Parviz Mehri, Washington University (St. Louis)," or "Joe Sambursky, Binghampton, but I grew up in Brazil." And selected out of 500 applicants, they could start seeing eye patients before they knew any ophthalmology. Why not?

It was one day during that first week when Miss Goshorn, beautiful Miss Goshorn, who had been chief nurse in the East Eye Clinic for twenty years, came out of the dark room where the microscope exams were done, walked up to me and said, "We have a problem. Something seems to be wrong with Dr. Reid." Pete Reid, little guy, always seemed to be chomping a cigar, introduced to me just a few days before with, "Hi, Pete Reid here, from South Berwick Maine." I had been happy to make his acquaintance, I didn't need the localization, he was obviously from "down Maine" as is said in that part of New England. I had not had a real chance to get to know him up to that point.

I said to Miss Goshorn, "What's wrong?"

She related a patient had come out of the dark room and said, "I think there is something wrong with my doctor; he just sits looking into the microscope, and it's been several minutes." The patient had realized something was wrong, she on one end of the microscope with her chin on the chin rest, Pete Reid on the other looking through the binoculars-and staying there for minutes, not moving, not talking.

I walked in to the room and there was Pete, slouched forward, essentially with his head propped up against the microscope by his orbital bones, more exactly the frontal bones making up the roof of the orbits. I gently moved him away, he was only semi conscious, and with the help of another resident I lay him on the floor. Miss Goshorn turned on the lights. I could see his face was slightly gray—more important, his skin felt moist, clammy. His pulse was present, rapid, but weak. I knew nothing of any past medical history with him, I only knew his name, Pete actually, I had forgotten the Reid. But I had not forgotten medical school, and certainly not my recent internship.

I shouted, "Go get me a syringe of glucose." A crowd of doctors (residents) and nurses gathered around, Pete on the floor of the clinic, me hovering over him. Within a minute or two, a nurse arrived with a 4-inch syringe filled with glucose.

I took it from her just as one of the second-year residents in Ear, Nose and Throat shouted, "What are you doing? You can't do that."

I looked up at him and said, "And why not? He is having an insulin reaction. He is in shock, get out of my way."

He said, "If you give him the shot we won't know what his blood sugar level was. We won't know what was wrong with him. We have to get a blood sugar level first." This from a second-year resident in ENT, essentially senior to me. My own second-year resident, who also had been in the clinic, had seen I was taking care of the emergency so he had left the hospital to go to the bank around the corner, lunch hour, he had to make a withdrawal. I was in charge. I looked at the ENT resident obstructing me.

I was only a first year eye resident, just out of my internship. Did I have the nerve to counter the dictate of a second-year man? I had the syringe in one hand, a tourniquet in the other. I said, "No? Just watch!" as I put the rubber tourniquet on Pete's right arm, found a vein, inserted the needle from the syringe, released the tourniquet, and pumped in the whole syringe full of glucose."

Within seconds Pete Reid opened his eyes, looked at me and said, "What happened?"

"You had an insulin reaction, Pete, how do you feel?"

"Yeah, I'm diabetic. I'm okay."

As astonishing event as it was—here is the sequel that is even more incredible. The second-year eye resident, Ed Trainer, who figured I could take care of a medical emergency okay and had gone to the bank, returned about ten minutes after the incident. He came to me, hurriedly, and related the following—in line in the bank he had struck up a conversation with the young man ahead of him, told him he was a resident at the Manhattan Eye and Ear. Whereupon the young man related his brother had just started his residency there, what a coincidence, and said, "His name is Pete Reid." Ed Turner suddenly realized this young man's brother, Pete Reid, was the one with the medical emergency back in the clinic.

"Does he have any medical issues, your brother?"

"Oh, yes, he has diabetes."

Ed raced back to the clinic, ran to me and yelled, "He has diabetes; he has diabetes."

I told him, "Thanks, I knew that."

Peter Reid Jr. completed his residency with distinction, chomping on his cigar all the way, and arguing his conservative politics with his New York friends who loved him nonetheless, took his growing family to live and practice ophthalmology in Exeter, New Hampshire, close enough to the down east Maine he so dearly loved. He practiced ophthalmology for 20 years and died of cardiac complication of diabetes in his fifties.

Silence in the Operating Room

I was still on active duty in the U.S. Navy, at U.S. Hospital #59, St. Albans, NY. In 1964—at the time of the beginning of war in southeast Asia, casualties coming in from Laos and Cambodia, before the full blown Vietnam War. We took care of 500 dependent families in the Greater New York area—Navy, Army, Air Force and Marines, plus the casualties in need of surgery on injured eyes from overseas. When an injured armed service member from overseas needed surgery he or she could ask to be sent to whatever military hospital in the country he or she wanted. We were busy in the clinic and in the operating room. Some people think I only played tennis in the Navy. Not so, I only played a few weeks of the year—when the All Navy championships and the interservice matches were held, the rest of the time I was a very busy eye surgeon, with just one partner to share the work in the eye department. We did have a civilian consultant, Dr. John McLean, chief of ophthalmology at NY Hospital Cornell Medical School, but he only came out to St. Albans once a month to examine our problem cases with us and advise about surgery. He was a brilliant physician and surgeon, and his opinion was like an order from God, like an automatic prescription. When he said we should consider surgery we would have the patient scheduled in the OR for the next morning.

I left active duty in 1965, and after a year of post graduate fellowship training in eye muscle disorders, my eventual subspecialty, I returned to New York City to assume the position of resident instructor at the Manhattan Eye, Ear and Throat Hospital where I had trained as a resident myself.

In fact, John McLean stepped down as civilian consultant to the Navy hospital and I was asked to become the new consultant, which I was happy to do and did so for some years after. He continued his work as chief at New York Hospital and Cornell Medical School and the following year he asked me to come on the staff at the hospital and on the faculty of the medical school and to direct the eye muscle department. Of course I accepted, although it meant a clinic a week at both Manhattan Eye and Ear, and NY Hospital, operating with the residents at both hospitals twice a week, and attending Grand Rounds at both hospitals weekly. I was young, I was up for it.

A year after I came on board at Cornell-NYH, one of Dr. McLean's most brilliant students had been awarded the position of chief of ophthalmology at the Flower and Fifth Avenue Hospital and named Professor at NY Medical College, its affiliate medical school. Dr. Miles Galin, the new young chief proceeded to amass a staff of bright, young eye surgeons to his faculty. He asked me to join him at NY Medical College.

Not thinking anything wrong in accepting his offer, I accepted. It was probably less than a week before I got a call from Dr. McLean at NY Hospital, summoning me to his office. He could be very forbidding at times. In fact, most of the staff was terrified of him. He had always been cordial to me; however, warmth I would say was not his forte.

We sat down and he got right to the point. "Do you know the rule about being on the staff of more than one medical school in New York City?"

I said I did not.

He enlightened me. "No one can be on the staff of more than one medical school in New York City at one time—unless you are the county coroner—the medical examiner for New York City" (gulp) "And," he added with the cool slightly sarcastic tinge for which he was known, "Your name is not Milton Helperin." (Dr. Milton Helperin was of course the county coroner, the medical examiner of New York City, professor of pathology at New York University Medical School, and on the staff of all five, at the time, medical schools in the city." (gulp again). What he was saying in not as many words was Cornell Medical School or NY Medical College. Take your pick. I stayed at Cornell.

I operated at Cornell-NYH and also at Manhattan Eye and Ear and did private cases as well as assisted the residents at both. My home of course had been Manhattan Eye and Ear where I had trained so I had more familiarity and warmth with both medical staff and nursing staff there. NY Hospital could be a bit cold. There were, however, some giants in medicine and surgery there, and not just in ophthalmology or ENT. One of the brightest luminaries in my time was the very famous neurosurgeon, Dr. Bronson Ray. He was a pioneer in surgery of the pituitary gland, and performed more hypophysectomies (ablations of the pituitary gland) in his day probably than anyone else in the world. The saying was, "A pituitary a day with Bronson Ray. (The residents would say "a hypophysectomy a day with Bronson Ray.") He was brilliant, and no one to be trifled with, as were many chiefs of surgery, whatever specialty, especially brain surgery.

It is said that once he stopped his car to help someone injured in an auto accident and as he started to help, a young boy pushed his way through the crowd and brushed Dr. Ray, saying, "Watch out, watch out, I will take over, I'm a Boy Scout."

Dr. Ray moved him aside and said, "That's okay, I'm a Scoutmaster."

Visiting neurosurgeons came from far and wide to observe him operate on a pituitary gland at NY Hospital. He welcomed them but there was one inviolate rule: absolute silence in the OR. And always observed. It is said that one time Dr. Ray's chief resident was helping him do an operation, one Victor Marshall, who eventually shifted to urology and became one of the most noted urologic surgeons in the world. But when he was in surgical training at NY Hospital and assisting Dr. Ray in neurosurgery, Dr. Ray was his idol. It is said that one time when Victor Marshall was assisting Bronson Ray do a hypophysectomy a little old man was standing in the OR observing from behind Dr. Marshall and Dr. Ray. Dr. Marshall took no note of him until unbelievably, and without any warning, a voice was heard to break the silence in the room. "Suck a little over there," it said. Victor was in shock, he turned his head to see where the voice came from, and when he turned back to the operating field, there was Dr. Ray using the suction tip on some blood where the direction of the voice seemed to suggest. A few minutes later the silence was broken again, only this time the voice said, "Cook a little over there." Victor wheeled around and saw the little old man pointing to a spot in the operative field, only to turn back and see Bronson using the Bovie electrocautery to coagulate a blood vessel—right where the old man had pointed. This happened once more, the counsel again being, "Cook a little over there," with Dr. Ray doing just that.

Finally Victor Marshall could stand it no longer, his idol Bronson Ray tolerating, and accepting, advices from this little old unknown visitor. Victor Marshall said to Dr. Ray, "Bronson, Bronson, tell me the word, and I will kick that guy out of the operating room."

Dr. Bronson Ray, leader of the field of neurosurgery at the time, said under his breath, "Shut up, you crazy bastard, that's Harvey Cushing." So it is said.

Note: Dr. Harvey Cushing is known as the father of modern neurosurgery. He was the principal teacher of neurosurgery in the United States in the first decades of the 20th Century. He developed with the physicist Bovie the Bovie electocautery to close bleeding blood vessels in brain operations. His name is famous for having first described Cushing's disease, a growth in the pituitary gland of the brain.

Watch One, Do One, Teach One

I interned in 1959 at the Lenox Hill Hospital in New York City in what was a neighborhood called Yorkville, or Germantown, on the east side of town, between Park Avenue and Third, roughly from 72nd Street to 96th Street. Before it became Lenox Hill it was called the *deutschekrankenhaus* (the German Sickhouse). And as interns we were quartered on the roof of the hospital's Ana Orfendorfer Clinic on Park Avenue and 76th Street. When asked we would always say we lived "on Park Avenue." It was a rotating internship (we rotated through all the medical specialties), and it was there I had my first exposure to ophthalmology. I saw a cataract extraction for the first time and immediately said, "Aha! This is why I slaved those four years in medical school having no idea why I was there." I immediately set out to secure a residency in ophthalmology, but I was very late in the process. Some of my fellow interns, having known they wanted ophthalmology while in medical school, (Lenox Hill attracted future ophthalmologists) already had positions. They laughed at me for thinking I might obtain one so late in the process.

My father, who was an orthopedist in Long Island City in Queens, across the river from Manhattan, told me to go see Guernsey Frey if I really wanted ophthalmology, disappointed I was not going into orthopedics like him. Dr. Guernsey Frey was a Scotsman, very proper, a thin gray moustache, he wore spats on his shoes, sported a silver-tipped cane, a black homburg hat, and a velvet-collared overcoat. He was very waspy. He was a surgeon director at the Manhattan Eye Ear and Throat Hospital on 64th Street, the most prestigious eye hospital in the city, and one of the most renowned in the country. A residency there would mean superb training as an eye surgeon besides opportunities for practice following graduation. Only six residents per year out of about 500 applicants, the selections always made one year before a student graduated from medical school. Not to mention that no women were ever selected, and rarely a minority candidate, especially a Jewish one. So my fellow interns laughed at me. My father was friends with Guernsey Frey Sr. who was in the general practice of medicine and who had started out in the 1920s visiting his patients in the farmlands of Astoria in Queens by horse and buggy. My father figured, correctly, that Guernsey Sr. would help out. When I met Guernsey Jr. at the

Manhattan Eye and Ear he said, "So you want to do ophthalmology? Okay, you can start in the group coming in July." I told my father, who was not all that impressed. But when I told my fellow interns they nearly fell on the floor. Evidently a prospective resident had dropped out, and I came along at the right time.

Before I came there I didn't even know Lenox Hill attracted so many prospective ophthalmologists. I chose it because it was a rotating internship in New York City, and also because my father was friends with Sydney Gaynor, the orthopedist for the NY Yankees baseball team and I was considering orthopedics, or at least, respecting my father's wish for me, trying it out. I assisted Sydney in the operating room a few times, and he encouraged me to orthopedics. So did James Nicholas, whom I also assisted, who later became famous as the NY Jets football orthopedist, and the inventor of the Namath knee brace for their famous quarterback Joe Namath. The hospital was also famous for having celebrities as patients, one of the reasons for that being Mortimer Rodgers, a well-known obstetrician and gynecologist—and brother of Richard Rodgers. I remember while I was there Andre Kostelanetz, the music composer; Richard Rodgers, the composer of Broadway musicals with his partner Lorenz Hart; even Marilyn Monroe—that caused quite a stir amongst the housestaff—and of course several ballplayers including Joe DiMaggio and Mickey Mantle. But our most famous guest of all was General Douglas MacArthur, for whom an entire wing was closed off, in order to get him in shape for his prostate operation by Dr. William Slaughter—yes, that was his surgeon's name. So secure was the general's stay, which was for weeks, that only the chief resident in medicine, Stu Sofferman, was allowed to draw his blood for lab work every day. No lowly intern like me, who usually did all the "scut work," was allowed near the general. The same Stu Sofferman by the way who would keep me up for hours, depriving me of the occasional forty winks interns could get for sleep; our shifts were round the clock, playing ping pong for money with me in the interns and residents quarters above the clinic. I would have to let him finally win a game so I could catch a few hours of sleep.

One of the several of the illustrious Lenox Hill medical staff was the chief of chest surgery, Dr. Herbert Meier. He was very foreboding, the residents and interns terrified in his presence, and I had little to do with him, being a lowly intern and not one of his surgical staff. But Lenox Hill was not large and sometimes even the lowly interns would assist chest surgery, even neurosurgery.

I remember once assisting for the first time the one neurosurgeon on the staff—Juan Negrin—do an ablation of the pituitary gland in a case of Cushing's disease, and while scrubbing at the sink before surgery Dr. Negrin said to me, "So, how many craniotomies have you scrubbed in on?"

I replied, "Sir, this is my first one."

Whereupon he threw his scrub brush into the air and screamed, "They send me a junior assistant intern to do a craniotomy."

I sweetly replied, "Dr. Negrin, I am not a junior assistant intern, but I will do the best I can to assist."

But I must not digress, back to Dr. Meier. I don't remember scrubbing with him, but I do remember making rounds at the bedside with him one time when we came upon a clinic patient who had just died early that morning.

I was somewhat surprised when Dr. Meier said to the assembled residents and interns, "Watch, I am going to demonstrate opening the chest and doing cardiac massage, in case any of you have to do it one day." This of course was 1959, no closed chest massage, no defibrillator back then. He proceeded to make a longitudinal incision along the upper border of one of the ribs that attached to the sternum on the left side of the chest, explaining the blood vessels were situated at the lower border of the ribs. Then he slid his hand between the ribs, spreading them apart, felt for the pleural cavity—pleura and lungs, and then the heart covered by pericardium and with the great blood vessels attached—arteries and veins. He squeezed the heart repeatedly and demonstrated a palpable pulse in the neck. That was it. Dramatic? Amazing? Heartless? It was a lesson we didn't expect. And wondered why he did it.

When I arrived in July at the Manhattan Eye Ear and Throat Hospital to begin my training as a first-year resident in ophthalmology I knew I had had a good experience as an intern, I could manage diabetes, take care of most medical emergencies, workup a patient for surgery, and manage medical complications. I was now eager to learn how to do cataract surgery. The first-year residents were assigned to assist on eye surgery—mostly eye muscle operations, orbital procedures, and even get to do a few of the less desirable operations like enucleations and eviscerations. Assisting on cataracts was for the second-year residents mostly. For this reason I would sometimes just go into the operating room to observe cataract surgery, especially to watch the leaders in the field, whenever I had the time. One time I was observing cataract surgery on a 21-year-old woman, very young to have cataracts, but she had juvenile diabetes which contributed to cataract development.

The operation was under general anesthesia, as was not unusual at the time, especially for a young patient. I was excited to be observing, the surgeon was the venerable Dr. Joseph Laval, chief of ophthalmology at Mt. Sinai Hospital. He did most of his cataracts at the Manhattan Eye and Ear. The top eye surgeons in New York City were—in no particular order—the chief at Columbia, the chief at Cornell, and the one Jewish chief at Mt. Sinai. The operation started without incident, the patient was intubated with an endo tracheal tube, fully unconscious, the resident helping Dr. Laval had prepped and draped, leaving only the small opening in the drape to expose the eye, Dr. Laval seated behind the patient's head. He wore his magnifying loupes, no microscope back then, and no gloves. It was an informal rule, the 30-year rule, if you operated for 30 years you didn't have to wear gloves anymore. Actually it meant, in his case, his surgical technique was so rigorous, so fastidious, that his fingers never came near the eye, only his instruments, which were sterilized of course, touched the eye. There was little likelihood of contamination of the operative field. I think the 30-year rule was retired when old Joe Laval retired. The assisting resident sat on the side of the operated eye, the anesthesiologist, Englishman Cyril Sanger sat by his anesthesia machine close by. I stood behind Dr. Laval, the better to get a good view of his surgical technique. I felt privileged to be there.

Within a minute of the start of surgery—I think the resident had just inserted the wire speculum, which spread the eyelids apart—I heard Dr. Sanger, in his understated calm voice say, "I am not getting a pulse." And a moment later, "I am not getting a blood pressure." Muted quiet Cyril Sanger, he who drove a British Rover automobile and not a Cadillac or a doctor's Buick, repeated, "I have no pulse."

I remember Dr. Laval looking over his loupes at Dr. Sanger, and bellowing, "Is she dead?" Whereupon Dr. Sanger turned to the wall of the operating room a few feet behind him and reached for the scalpel affixed by Scotch tape on the wall, taking it in his hand and saying quietly, "I believe we have to open the chest…" He looked first at Dr. Laval, then at his resident, then at me. He handed me the scalpel, finishing his sentence, "Dr. Raskind."

I do not remember any conscious thoughts from that moment until a few minutes later. But I do remember what I did. I took the scalpel from him, I pulled back the drape, I felt for a rib on the left side of the chest, and made a longitudinal incision along the upper border of the rib, spread the ribs apart, inserted my hand into the chest cavity. I didn't break any ribs. I have a strong grip but a thin wrist. I felt for the pleura covering the lung, moved the lung aside, and felt for the heart, which I began to squeeze rhythmically, forcefully. I stopped for a few moments and heard Cyril Sanger say, "I have a pulse." I waited, my hand still around the heart, not squeezing. He repeated, "I have a pulse," and then, "I am getting a blood pressure."

I did not know how I knew how or what I had done. I simply came to the realization I was standing over a 21-year-old patient with my hand in her chest. I said in a calm voice to the scrub nurse standing by, "Please call Donald Wood Smith and ask him to come up and help me close the chest." Donald Wood Smith, an Aussie, was a post-graduate fellow in plastic surgery, trained in general surgery before his plastic training. He would know how to help.

When he arrived at the operating room he poked his head in the door and said, "Dicko, what are you doing with your hand in that bloody girl's chest?"

I replied, "Just scrub and come in here and help me close this thing." Which he did. There had been no hemorrhage in the pericardium, nor the pleura, nor the chest wall. The patient made an uneventful recovery, cataract surgery postponed for another time. On the following morning, Dr. Laval took me to the private room where the young woman was recovering, more like a hotel room, chaise lounges for the family near the hospital bed, a view out over the east side of Manhattan, many of his patients very wealthy New Yorkers.

He brought me in and introduced me to the patient and her parents. I don't even know her name. He said, "This is the young doctor who saved your life."

"I'm with you, Mr. Coles."

In order to protect the innocent I changed some names in stories I wrote years ago and George was called Josh. But his real name was George, and since he's no longer with us and he has almost no living relatives I now prefer to call him by his rightful name, which I should because he was a true friend of mine through high school until his death in 1985, notwithstanding he had a strange way of showing it.

He was my alter ego, in a way, always telling me I couldn't do the impossible things I had every intention of doing. The most important, of course, was that I was going to change my sex, and he put every conceivable, diabolical, annoying, disruptive, obstacle in the way of that eventuality taking place, until ultimately when it had become a "*fait accompli*" he realized the futility of his task. Although it was I who did the most outrageous deed with "the big change" it was actually George who did many smaller deeds of some absurdity, the big difference being that what I did was to myself, what George would do was to others. Maybe I unconsciously admired some of them, things I would never do myself.

He was brought up in the Bronx—in the University Heights section near NYU, "uptown division"—in a small frame house, in a row of small frame houses, which served also as his father's office for the general practice of medicine. George's room on the second floor was tiny, and even though he had not reached the full six feet five, two hundred eighty-plus pounds of his adulthood, he was big even in high school. I would visit him for an overnight sometimes back then, our high school—the Horace Mann School for Boys, in the Riverdale section of the Bronx—much closer to George's home than mine. I even played stickball for his team, Harrison Avenue, against others from neighboring street sections of the Bronx.

George, his bed, and his monstrous stereo hi-fi set, the size of a modern refrigerator, filled up his entire room. He was big, even in "second form" (eighth grade in the old English prep school classification) and wore very thick glasses. He was not the more attractive figure he ultimately became in adulthood, when he shed his glasses for contact lenses.

I met him the first time one day when I brought my Kodak Bantam camera to school and gave a talk to the class about photography and demonstrated my Bantam, especially the feature it had of being able to self-time a picture on a delay, so that the photographer could run quickly and get into the picture. It would go "bzzzzz" for a few seconds and then the shutter would trip. George and Ray Chen were intrigued and came up to me after the class. That started a friendship between the three of us, which continued for a lifetime.

George was larger than the other kids in our class, but not more powerful, having not yet developed strong muscles. He was bullied by a few of our classmates and it was good I was his friend as I was a popular member of the class. He was just big...big all over, even a big face. Even his lips were big. Awful, the bullies called him liver lips. He was a good friend, but even I do admit he was not a very attractive youngster. His fine motor coordination for things like model airplanes or hi-fi radio kits was okay, but he wasn't a particularly good athlete either.

He didn't really fit in in our class of mostly excellent students and athletes, rather sophisticate sons of upper-middle-class New York City (Manhattan) parents. Those of us who were a little bit intellectual, like Ray Chen and me, and a few of the other smarter students in the class—who didn't really care how handsome, well-dressed or athletic one was—befriended George. George and Ray and I struck up a friendship based mostly on intellectual interests, Ray and I shared other interests as well—sports and even the classics.

George had a very high IQ, but he never quite achieved in his professional life his full potential. He worked only as hard as he had to in school. For example, we learned "logarithms in mathematics class, shorthand in order to multiply large numbers. He didn't bother with learning how to do the logarithms; he would just multiply by long hand the long string of numbers. Of course he would often do better than those of us did with the logarithms; we made some mistakes along the way. But we had learned a new skill and he didn't. He was clever, most of us were not.

He was as quick with his tongue as he was with his mind. He would pass judgment on our classmates and on our teachers with no censorship, his criticism and his sarcasm biting. He also brooked no patience with stupidity. He was a great mimic, and he would mimic a classmate's foibles to a T, accompanied by vocal inflection and facial grimace. He should have been a comedian in the Catskill mountain resorts in upstate New York—the "Jewish Alps," the "Borscht Belt" it was called. And he loved to play jokes. One time he went up to the famous comedian from the "mountains," Barry Levinson, and tried to embarrass him, to convince him he was an old friend whom Barry had forgotten. Finally Barry looked at him and said, "Oh, yeah, I know you. You're that wise guy from Fire Island," putting George, for that once, in his place. George would call people on the telephone and say something ridiculous, or make believe he was somebody else. He was deadly behind the screen of a telephone.

He was a prankster for sure, but he had a diabolic side as well. One of the worst things he ever did was to get some picric acid from the chemistry laboratory, which had the smell of someone throwing up, vomiting; it was horrible. He brought a tiny little vial of it to the candy store near where he lived, where the owner had caught him pinching candy and barred him from coming back. He dropped a few drops of this picric acid on the floor at the entry way to the poor man's store and then ran out the door. It was about three days before anyone could enter that store, because of the horrible smell of emesis, no matter how hard the poor guy scrubbed the floor.

George did several things less horrible than that, but still typified his sometimes diabolical side. There was a big hill going up to the school at Horace Mann, (it's still there of course) and we trudged up from the end of the line, the last stop, of the subway (elevated above ground by the time it reached 242nd Street). In fact, the school's nickname used to be The Hill Toppers. In winter, George would get up the hill to school early and start hurling ice balls down on the students coming up from the subway below to go to school. Although he wasn't a very accurate pitcher in his short-lived career on the junior varsity baseball team, he was uncanny with ice balls—ice balls raining down on the students trudging up the hill in their galoshes and their mackinaws (plaid wool checkered overcoats) and their suitcases full of books. We didn't have backpacks in those days, just a big book bag, which one carried by a little handle. It weighed you down on one side, with all the books we had to study you had to shift it to the other arm from time to time. It was a steep and long trek up that hill and a teacher would have to come out and call George off so classes could begin because he was so deadly with those ice balls. When he would see me coming up the hill, however, he would stop and I would be allowed to proceed to get to school.

We used to go to baseball games at Yankee Stadium, and sometimes at the Polo Grounds, with Larry Van Gelder, another Horace Mann student, who ended up the movie reviewer for *The New York Times*. Van, as he was called, used to go to the NY Giants games in the old Polo Grounds in a Giants uniform and bring his baseball glove as well. This was in the old days, before it was common for kids to wear uniform jerseys of their favorite players and to bring baseball gloves into the stadium. He had a complete Giants uniform: hat, shirt, pants, socks, baseball shoes and glove.

We all went to camp together at Camp Moosilauke in New Hampshire. George and Larry Van Gelder and my friend Dan Danneman worked in the ice house to make a little spending money. That made it very easy to get as much ice cream as we wanted, because the ice cream was stored in the ice house. Occasionally George and I used to go fishing at five o'clock in the morning, with Dan and Joe Waters, the camp cook, who was black (no one said African American back then). Joe would bring his pistol, a .38 caliber revolver, along. I don't think George or Dan had ever seen an actual pistol before. Joe never shot it at anybody. It was just for safety, he said. What he was being safe from, at five in the morning on Upper Baker Pond, Orford, New Hampshire? We never really found out. Sometimes I went out on the lake alone—not at five in the morning—looking for Connie Chase way over on the far end. George would stand on the camp side of the lake yelling, "Rastus! Rastus! Get back in the kitchen and cook up the grub, Rastus." George was trying to make Connie Chase's father think some black kid who worked in the camp kitchen was coming across the lake after his daughter. I implored him to cease this stupid, dangerous joke. "Pug" Chase could have just as soon taken aim with his rifle at me in the rowboat, but George managed to do it every time I would try to sneak across the lake.

We lost track of each other after high school, because he stayed in the city and went to Columbia University, while I went off to Yale in Connecticut. In fact, he never left the city—public school in the Bronx, Horace Mann, Columbia, NYU Medical School, Mt. Sinai Hospital, Manhattan Eye and Ear Hospital. Unlike me, I was off all over the country and the world to pursue my education. George was a through and through New Yorker.

He used to spend an inordinate amount of time on the phone (no cell phones back then). Because he wasn't so good-looking, he could hide behind the telephone. He would call models and be very engaging, gregarious, and charming to them, and he would carry on telephone romances, more than actual, true encounters. (Not so different from the modern day on the Internet I do realize.) Rarely he got lucky and did manage a few actual dates. He was very persistent. His principle was if you try 100 times, as they say, you may score on one or two of them. So different from me. One rejection would put me into a depression. George was not shy, and he would go after all the top models in New York—Eileen Ford's group and Paris Planning and Wilhelmina's, all the top agencies. He had all their contact sheets, the pictures of the models. That's how I would meet some myself, through George. Sometimes I would take up with one of them after being introduced by him. I even met my son's mother that way, but that is a whole other story.

George and I went to Sweden one time and met several beautiful young Scandinavian girls. George felt I was a good decoy, or bait because there was something ominous about a single person going after all these young girls in a strange city, but if there were two young men, especially if one of them was good-looking, it made it easier. I remember we were in Stockholm on Hager Day, the day in 1966 that Sweden switched from driving on the left side of roads to the right. Thousands of pretty high school girls were stationed as temporary traffic cops to help pedestrians cross the street without getting killed, especially looking the wrong way at the roundabouts. George had a field day trying to meet all of them.

We resumed our friendship when I came back to New York City after medical school to become an intern at Lenox Hill Hospital, and then a resident in ophthalmology at the Manhattan Eye and Ear. We began a number of years as bachelor friends in New York City. George had a walk-up apartment on 52nd Street, off First Avenue, called a railroad flat, one room connected to another in a row, four flights up, top floor of a brownstone building, almost a tenement, which it probably had been before "The War."

He decorated it very nicely, on the cheap, despite his father having died after being in general practice in the family's house in the Bronx, and George had come upon about a half a million dollars in cash in his basement—all of the ten and twenty dollar fees for medical services for over half a century. He converted that first apartment into an indirect, off-lighted, somewhat sinister and erotically suggestive bachelor's pad—the better to lure a young model to bed.

We each had Chevrolet Corvette convertibles—1964, fuel-injected, 375 hp. George always had to keep up with me. I got a Maserati, he had to have one. I got a Corvette, he had to have one. We drove them all over, speeding in and around the metropolitan area, with the top down, a gorgeous girl in the passenger seat when it was not inhabited by his Doberman Pinscher or my Airedale Terrier. He always had a Doberman and I always had an Airedale. If he got stopped by a cop for speeding, he would hold up an old syphilitic bottle of blood, of no use to the blood bank, and tell the cop he was on an emergency call to deliver blood to the hospital. That, plus the MD license plate always got him off. If he had outraced me down the Harlem River Speedway, the cop would catch up to me, with George escaping ahead. And we used to tinker with the engines too. He taught me a lot about automobile engines; he was very mechanical.

When I had my airplane in the late '60s, we would fly to the island of Martha's Vineyard off Cape Cod, Massachusetts or out to

Easthampton on Long Island. George never, ever considered I knew nothing about instrument flying. He would goad me into flying with zero visibility from the Vineyard to Easthampton over the Long Island Sound—we could just as easily flown out past Montauk Point into the ocean toward England for all he knew. And time and again I would accept his goading and almost get us killed. We would always have the two dogs with us, even in the airplane. We were inseparable with our dogs—me with my Airedale, Rocco, and George with his Doberman, Odin. Even took them into restaurants with us—PJ Clarke's Tavern on Third Avenue and Martell's further uptown were our favorites.

One time George took a shot at a man trying to steal his Corvette, parked on 52nd Street when its alarm went off and George leaned out of his fourth floor window and saw the culprit entering his car. He shot him. He wasn't a very good shot; the bullet just grazed the would-be thief's arm. The man yelped and made a beeline in the direction of the subway station. It's a good thing George didn't have better aim, or he would have killed him for sure.

Another time, we came upon a man in his parked Corvette, and when I saw him from about twenty feet away I started to yell because I didn't want George to get to the car while the man was still in it, George would certainly have tried to kill him too. My yelling worked, as we were running toward the car the man made it out and got away from George, in slow but hot pursuit.

One of the worst things George did to me was when I was beginning the change from Dick to Renée and George was pulling out all the stops to prevent that from happening. George knew the future Renée was all dressed to the nines and was going to go to one of the bars George and Dick (meaning my former 'me') used to frequent, Chuck's Composite—a very popular spot on the east side for the swinging singles of the day. George tipped off the bartender that the future Renée would be coming in that night.

When Renée—all dressed up and with a beautiful long auburn wig, heavy makeup, garish I am sure—came into the bar, the bartender gave Renée a very hard time, mocking her, insulting her, because he knew who she was. This was very disturbing to Renée, because she was hoping, in the early days of her transition, to pass and obviously she failed the test with the bartender, forewarned by George. That's the way he was. He wanted to keep his friend, Dick, as he knew him. Nevertheless, when Renée did finally emerge, as real, I must say George remained Renée's friend, just as close as he had been to Dick, maybe even closer.

One of the worst stories about George is actually a bit macabre. No, really, it was awful, and I participated in it. It took place when George was a resident at the Manhattan Eye and Ear Hospital, and Dick was in the Navy, stationed out at St. Alban's Naval Hospital, near the JFK airport. Dick had convinced George he should switch from general surgery to ophthalmology and helped him to obtain a residency at the Manhattan Eye and Ear. Dick had kept his apartment across the street from the hospital, and George was still living in his apartment on 52nd Street. George used to have his Doberman Pinscher, Odin, stay sometimes in Dick's apartment with Dick's dog, Rocco (although Rocco usually came with Dick out to St. Alban's Hospital). The two dogs were, on occasion, then, in that apartment, across the street from Manhattan Eye and Ear, alone. They were usually pretty well-behaved, but sometimes there would be some barking. Besides the fact Odin ate Rocco's bed one time, they were well-behaved dogs, big as they were, and both very friendly.

Some barking occurred enough times that one of the tenants in the apartment building objected to it and complained to the superintendent, who then complained to Dick that there was a lot of barking coming from his apartment. Unfortunately George found out the complaint came from old Mr. Fester, who lived in the apartment in the same line as Dick's, only two floors below. Now, how Mr. Fester was able to hear barking in an apartment two flights above him, I don't know, but he made the complaint and after George found out it was Mr. Fester he did a terrible thing to him.

Mr. Fester's life was hard enough, as it was, because he had a son who lived in the building with him, who was a grown man, who obviously had some psychiatric disorder, because whenever he got into the elevator, he would never face the people in the elevator car. He would stand in the corner facing the wall until he reached his floor and then silently exited. Here was this poor old man with troubles enough with his own son, who unfortunately crossed George and was about to feel his wrath.

One night, George and Dick were sitting in George's apartment on 52nd Street and the two dogs were with us. Dick's partment across from the hospital on 64th Street was vacant.

George called Mr. Fester on the telephone about midnight and said, "Mr. Fester, this is Mr. Coles. I live in Eleven C (which was an apartment in the same line as Dick's apartment and Mr. Fester's). I hear that you've been as upset as I have about these dogs barking."

And Mr. Fester said, "Oh, Mr. Coles. Yes, I'm very upset. I hear them barking all the time."

And then, George said, "Mr. Fester, I'm even hearing them barking now. Can you hear them barking now? Can you hear them barking right now?" (Of course, the two dogs were with us on 52nd Street.)

But Mr. Fester went to the door of his apartment and came back and said, "Mr. Coles, I think I can hear them. Yes, I think I can hear them barking right now."

Whereupon, George said, "Mr. Fester, this is what I think we have to do. We have to form a petition. And we're gonna form this petition and we'll have to get all the signatures on it."

Mr. Fester said, "Mr. Coles, I'm with you. I'm with you, Mr. Coles."

Whereupon, George said, "Now, the first part of the petition is going to say, 'No dogs in the building.'"

"I am with you, Mr. Coles," Mr. Fester said.

Whereupon George said, "And, of course, we have to say no cats. We can't have any dirty cats with litter boxes all over the place. Even though they don't make noise, they're dirty and there are litter boxes all over and people might get cat scratch fever."

"I'm with you, Mr. Coles."

Whereupon George said, "And we should also include birds. Birds. Parrots. Parakeets, Cockatiels. You can get psittacosis from birds. They're filthy, filthy animals."

"I'm with you, Mr. Coles."

Whereupon, George said, "And don't forget the fish. All those guppies. Those little dirty guppies. No fish in the building, either."

And Mr. Fester said, "I'm with you, Mr. Coles."

Whereupon George said, "Ferrets. We can't have any ferrets running round and round either."

And Mr. Fester repeated, "I'm with you, Mr. Coles."

Finally, George said, "Mr. Fester, come on up to my apartment and sign the petition now. We've got to get this thing going right away."

Now this was midnight and Mr. Fester, octogenarian, old bathrobe-clad Mr. Fester said to George on the phone: "What apartment is it, Mr. Coles?"

And George said, "Come up to Eleven C. I'll be waiting here and I'll have the petition here for you to sign it. Bye, Mr. Fester."

"Bye, Mr. Coles."

About 20 minutes elapsed, and George picked up the phone again, calling Mr. Fester, and he said, "Mr. Fester, this is Mr. Coles."

A moment of silence and then: "Mr. Coles...Don't you ever call this number again, Mr. Coles. Don't you ever call this number again."

George had a brilliant mind, but besides the diabolical side he liked to live on the edge of disaster. One time, he got his hands on a blue box. This was still decades before cell phones. A blue box was the size of a modern cell phone, maybe a little thicker. It was an electronic device devised by a Chinese graduate student in electrical engineering, a device that could reproduce the sound of coins dropping into a coin-operated telephone booth. The quarter made a certain sound, the dime made a certain sound, the nickel made a certain sound. With this blue box, one could make long distance calls all over the world and not have to pay for them. You could call Florida for the weather. You could call Europe. You could call anywhere. George was intrigued by the blue box so he got one from this Chinese student.

I don't know how it happened, but after months of George bringing up Swedish models to his apartment and letting them call their mothers in Stockholm for free, he got caught. One day, there was a knock on his door and two men standing there identified themselves as FBI.

"Are you Dr. Klar?"

"Yes, sir."

"Do you have a blue box?"

"Doesn't everybody have one," said George, nervously chuckling.

"No, they don't and you are under arrest."

Well, by this time, George had moved to his posh bachelor apartment on the 26th floor, uptown on 85th Street with a terrace overlooking the northeast corner of the city, overlooking Third Avenue. It was a very sexy den of a New York bachelor pad, befitting the girls he trouped in and out. However, it looked like all the debauchery had come to an end on that night because George was arrested for illegal interstate traffic and he was up for a felony conviction. A felony conviction would mean the loss of his license to practice medicine, being kicked out of the hospital, a stiff jail term, and a monetary penalty in the thousands.

George was not the only object of the FBI's investigation. They were looking for the designer of the blue boxes, the Chinese graduate student who made them. So before they hauled George off to jail, they stationed an FBI man in his apartment to monitor all his phone calls in the hopes of finding more information. Another FBI man was on his roof, another stationed in the lobby. They intercepted all the calls that came in to his phone and questioned anyone visiting from the outside. During the surveillance a telephone call came in and there happened to be two FBI men in his apartment at the time.

One of them picked up the phone while the other one sat by, saying, "Who was it? Who was it? Who called?"

The partner replied, "You won't believe this, but it's Governor Carey."
At the time, Hugh Carey was governor of the State of New York, and he was calling George, who was his ophthalmologist, asking for some contact lenses George had promised him.

That was the kind of case it was. He was an ophthalmologist of some repute (actually George was the first one to bring soft contact lenses to America from Czechoslovakia, and ultimately he made a lot of money on Bausch and Lomb stock options; B+L was the manufacturer of the contacts in the USA). George had patients like Governor Carey. The FBI man was monitoring his calls to find the Chinese student who designed the blue boxes, and he discovers Governor Carey calling his ophthalmologist.

Anyway, George obtained the services of my good friend, Robert Cohen. Robert is still noted for being the top, or nearly one of the top, matrimonial lawyers in the country, but in this instance he was called upon to defend George, who was at risk of losing his ability to earn his living because of his kicks from making free long-distance calls for prospective dates with beautiful models. Robert went to work.

He said to the NY district attorney, "Look, this man has a little bit of a screw loose. He is not making any money from these blue boxes. He's not using it to make an illicit living. He's doing it because it's a little bit of a wild side of him that's a little bit nutty. He's doing it as a plaything. So, you have to reduce the charge from a felony to a misdemeanor or something lesser, because you have to make the punishment fit what actually the crime had been." He got him off. Because there was nothing in between a felony and nothing that was appropriate, he got him off. Got him off scott-free. They dropped the charges.

The ironic part of the story is George was furious at Robert for charging him $4,000 to get him off. He said, "What did he do? The stupid jerk. All he did was make a phone call."

As he matured, George became much more attractive than he had been as a youngster. He learned to dress better. He had contact lenses instead of his thick glasses. He had some interesting friends and he had a wonderful girlfriend who lived with him for many years in his farm in Connecticut. He practiced ophthalmology on Park Avenue, having taken over the practice of a well-respected ophthalmologist who had been the eye doctor for *The New York Times*. (I introduced the two of them to each other.)

Immediately after the "Big Change" (as some of my friends called my sex change) George accepted me as Renée. As soon as he realized his Herculean efforts to stave off the inevitable operation were to fail, even after having introduced Dick to his future wife, he turned around and Renée became his close friend, just as Dick had been his close friend before.

One might have thought George—who had been so vocal and so active in trying to prevent Renée's emergence, and tried so hard to preserve Dick—might be one who would just say, "That's it," and never again maintain the friendship. He didn't ,and many Sundays Renée would drive up to his farm in Connecticut and sit around the kitchen table with George and other assembled friends. It became a Sunday ritual for a few of us. Renée's friendship with George had little to do with sports, as it did most of her other long associations—tennis, golf, baseball, whatever. He didn't particularly like spectator sports and he wasn't a participant in golf or tennis. I don't even think he did much swimming in the pond at the farm in Connecticut. He liked working with his backhoe on his property and working in his shop, and doing things with his hands to fix up his house and his farm. He had a beautiful shop, immaculate, in his barn behind the house, and his stereophonic sound system had a wonderful speaker system belting out Bach and Brahms all day in the barn, while George worked with his tools.

He kept up the interest in cars for only a short time until he graduated to pickups and backhoes, but he did have a replica of a 1930 Model A Ford, which he bequeathed to me when he ultimately died in 1985. He got cancer of the colon probably because of all the cigarettes and Ballantine ales he drank in his lifetime—only about a carton of non-filtered Camels and about four six-packs of Ballantine Ale every day.

He discovered the mass in his abdomen himself and, when he went to the surgeon at New York Hospital, the doctor walked in and said, "Oh, you're the doctor with the lump in the right side of the abdomen?" and George said, "No, sir. I'm the doctor with the cancer of the ascending colon." And, of course, that's exactly what he had. He was operated on, but it was too late. It had spread to his liver. He was on chemo a while and he quit that and finally said, "To hell with it."

Just before he died, he married his long-time girlfriend. He'd never been married in his whole life—he was 55. We had the ceremony on the property of the house I was building in Putnam County. The house hadn't been finished, but we had the ceremony on the hill looking down to the lake, the town justice of the peace presiding.

Shortly before his death, he asked both me and David Sudarsky, another good friend, famous retina surgeon whose country home was close by George's, to help him if he needed it. He didn't want to die an agonizingly painful death. He had given up the chemotherapy. He wasn't religious. I think he didn't have any religious sense of an afterlife at all. In fact, I know he didn't. He was convinced this was his one time to go around on this earth and that was it. He asked David and me to make sure he didn't suffer.

I obtained enough morphine to put George and all three of the horses in his barn asleep for a very long time. I intended to use it if I had to, but I didn't, because Sandy, his wife, called me one night and said George was having trouble breathing. I told her I would come over. A moment later she called back. She said he had just vomited about two pints of blood and dropped dead on the floor.

The last thing I remember him saying to me had been a few days before, when I visited him at the farm, "I hope I make it to the weekend. I'm reading a dynamite book and Tyson (heavyweight boxing champ Mike Tyson, whose career George had followed from the beginning) is fighting on Friday night." He didn't make it for the fight and he didn't finish the book.

It's curious. He used to pick on me unmercifully. I was the object of all his jibes and insults and I just took all his abuse and kept coming back for more because he was my friend and, although abuse me he would, I knew that just as staunchly he defended me to others. He was always mocking me that my feet were so big, and I was a lousy cook, and what a terrible woman I made, all kinds of insults. Maybe to others he extolled only my virtues, whatever they might be.

Why were we close friends? Almost ridiculous to say, but I think I appreciated his morality. He had a keen sense of right and wrong. Unfortunately when he felt wronged himself, he could extract retribution in ways beyond my comprehension. And of course his boldness socially was counterpoint to my bashfulness. I may have thought unconsciously of doing some of the dastardly deeds he actually did. Each lacked a few traits the other had.

One time, he said, in reference to me, "There, but for the grace of God, go I." And I never knew what he meant by that. I don't think he was a closet transsexual or a transvestite. Nor do I think he was gay. But he had something that made him identify with me in a very strong way. And so he said, "There, but for the grace of God go I."

"See what you did."

Amateur tennis and professional tennis are both played with a racquet, balls and a court with lines on it, but there are some big differences. Playing as a professional for one's livelihood is still a game, but the stakes are higher, the caliber of play is of course much better and the life of the participant quite different. I played as an amateur for most of my young life, in school, college, then on the amateur circuit, and then part-time in tournaments when I wasn't busy with my day job as an ophthalmologist. I was a true amateur sportsman as were many of us who combined earning a living in one career with participating seriously in another. When Open Tennis came in 1968, the distinction between amateur and professional became more defined. Some of the players who played the amateur circuit then became professionals, but most of them stayed amateurs, with a day job and a recreational career in addition.

Those of us who were good enough players to compete in sectional and national amateur events took the game seriously, in spite of not receiving any monetary gain for our efforts—a rare gold ball, a trophy, a ranking were our rewards for our efforts, besides the fun of competition and the camaraderie. There was another echelon of amateur player in the world of tennis too and still is, even after pro tennis came to be, and that is club tennis. In fact, by far there is more tennis played at clubs, recreational and competitive, than all the tennis played on tour, amateur or professional.

After school and college, if one wants to continue—or start, even—to play tennis, one does it at a club. The New York metropolitan area, where I lived on and off for decades, has several tennis clubs. Some of them are famous, like the West Side Tennis Club in Forest Hills, where the national championships and then the U.S. Open was held, the Seventh Regiment Tennis Club in the armory on Park Avenue, where the National Indoor Championships was held, and some not so famous, like the public club where I first picked up a racquet, chasing around after my father, picking up balls on dirt clay courts, or the Sunrise Tennis Club along the railroad tracks in Sunnyside Queens. Trains leaving Manhattan for points in Long Island first pass the world's largest railroad yard, the Sunnyside

Yards, and then make there way east through Queens into Nassau and points beyond. Because land next to a railroad track is cheap, many of the public, and some of the private, tennis club, were built with courts laid out in a row, parallel to the tracks. Even the famed West Side club in Forest Hills has most of its courts—not the stadium court of course—all in a row along the railroad tracks just before the station at Forest Hills. The great tennis champion Big Bill Tilden is famous for saying, "What train?" after a practice session with Little Bill Johnson when Little Bill said, "Sorry about those trains," which had come by throughout the practice.

The Great Neck Country Club was hardly that—a country club in the sense of manicured lawns, old world clubhouse, dining rooms, ballrooms, a place where the landed gentry could be among themselves for golf, tennis, croquet, dinner and drinks, lots of drinks. It was just a row of dirt clay courts along the railroad tracks in Great Neck, Long Island, near the train station. It had a tiny clubhouse and a shower, but almost none of the members changed there, most all lived within a half-hour car ride and would usually come dressed to play and go home that way. Nondescript as it appeared it had among its members some of the best tennis players in the metropolitan area— Bobby Riggs, the Fishbachs (Michael and Peter, who both played on the pro tour), Don Rubell, Paul Cranis, Bob Barker and me—all of us the top-ranked eastern men's players at one time or another, and some of us with national championships on our resume as well. We gravitated to Great Neck Country Club because the competition was good, one could always get a good game, the price for membership was cheap, and any and all were accepted for membership, including black, yellow or Semitic in origin. I was still living in my parent's home in Forest Hills, Queens, when I played at Great Neck, but I drove the twenty minutes there and back a few times a week. The West Side Tennis Club in Forest Hills, walking distance from my home, was still restricted—no Jews allowed. No blacks either, by the way. So Great Neck attracted the top area players, and every year we won the metropolitan club championship with no problem.

As with any club there was a broad spectrum of players' abilities. There were a few pros, some top amateurs, A and B class amateurs. This was in the day before a number system had been devised for players' abilities (1-5 as it is now). B players were pretty capable, useful they would say in England, but not tournament level. C players were more or less duffers, but no less enthusiastic than the top players. And just as competitive, just as ferocious. Doctors, lawyers, accountants, business men—they all took their tennis seriously. The club championships, A, B, C levels were always fiercely fought. One year when I won the club championship I beat a close friend—Bob Barker—we had beaten each other several times over the years, and a few years after I won that match he would win the national 35 and over singles title. As I said, the level of play at the club ranged from very high to beginner.

There was also a category of player not unique to Great Neck, but not common to all clubs—the doctors category. Great Neck had several physicians as members; some lived in Great Neck and practiced medicine in New York City. Some practiced locally. Because there were several doctors one year it was decided to hold a doctors championship along with the A and the B tournaments at the end of the season. And what I relate here in the following account was awful, and it was not Great Neck's proudest day, but I will relate it anyway.

At least I will not name names. I will simply call one doctor player Sam and the other John. This is what happened. In the semifinals of the doctors club championship Sam, a well-known internist in town, had to play John, an orthopedic surgeon who operated in New York. Sam and John had a long history. Pretty close in ability, they played often, but John always got the best of Sam. Well, they started to play the match in the tournament semifinal and Sam was having a good day. He even won the first set. He thought, "Finally I am going to beat John." It was in the second game of the second set when the phone rang in the clubhouse. It was for Sam, who yelled to the club member who took the call (no cell phones in those days, just a public telephone on the wall in the clubhouse). "Take a message." When the two players changed sides after the third game, Sam learned from the man who took the call that one of his patients in the hospital was having trouble breathing. So he ran in, called the hospital, and told the nurse in charge to give the patient some medication. He ran back to the court and resumed play. He had never beaten John. This was his chance.

After another game, he was still ahead by one game in the second set, another call came in. This time the message was, "She is still having trouble breathing."

At this point he turned to his opponent and said, "John, I have to go to the hospital. I have a patient in respiratory distress."

Whereupon John replies, "I understand, you have to go, but it's a default. You lose, I win."

Sam went nuts "You know what it's like. I have patient, I have to go."

And John repeated, "I understand, but it's a default. You lose, I win." Sam said they should continue the next day. John repeated that if he walked off the court the match was over.

Sam glared at him, and ran back to the phone: "Give her a shot of cortisone, I will be there soon." They went back to play, by now in the middle of the second set. Another call came, the patient still in distress, Sam once more telling John he had to go, John repeating he understood, but the match was over. Sam was beside himself. Another verbal order for more medicine, and they resumed play, dead even now in the second set, but still a chance for Sam to beat him for the first time.

At 5-5 in the set another call came and this time the messenger said, "Sam, you better take this one yourself."

Sam ran to the phone and heard the nurse report, "Your patient just expired." Sam turned ashen gray, sweating profusely, and pointed his finger at his opponent John, screaming for all the members, and a few passersby on the street to hear, "See what you did."

Club tennis in New York City—all over the country, the world—serious business.

The Corpsmen and the Lieutenant Commander

There is a difference between an LCD USN and an LCD USNR. The former is a career Naval officer, the latter a Navy Reserve, serving two years active duty and then six or more, whatever, on reserve. The real difference is the brass, and sometimes the non-coms too, understand the difference. A two-year active duty officer carries out the same duties as the careerist, but in the medical corps (MC) for example, it is evident a Navy doc who is USNR considers himself a doctor first and a Naval officer second. A careerist, even if he gets out on the day of his twenty-year stint, considers himself a Navy man first, a doctor second. Or so that's the way it seemed to me. At my hospital, our executive officer, the exec, surgeon, career Navy, hated me. I was a two-year man, and shortly became the most noted officer at the base, because the brass in Washington put me into some regional Navy tennis tournaments even before I had any indoctrination into Navy customs, as soon as I reported for active duty, July 1963, and then when I won them I was sent down to Bainbridge Naval Training Station, where I won the All Navy singles and doubles titles, and then they made me captain of the U.S. Navy Tennis Team—men, women, seniors.

The Navy Department sent a letter of commendation to Captain Yon, our commandant, congratulating him on having such a fine representation of a Navy officer on his base. Yon was bucking for admiral at the time and of course that didn't hurt, and by my second year of active duty Admiral Yon would always give me a smile and a brisk salute if we passed each other in the hallway. But the real reason the exec hated me was not just because I was a doctor first and Navy man second, it was because he lived on the grounds of the base, and my dog for some instinctive reason known only to him used the exec's lawn for his personal toilet. Dogs were not allowed on base, but everyone knew LCDR Raskind had a big Airedale Terrier in the front section of the barracks that served as the ophthalmology department and every time there was an inspection, the corpsmen in the eye department would make all gone with Rocco and with the bowl for water and the blanket and any other canine evidence so that when the inspectors, usually

Marines from the Brooklyn Navy Yard, came by all was spic and span, no kennel. It pissed off Capt. Wickmeyer to no end.

The corpsmen, to a man, and woman (one) were devoted to me. They were career Navy, but had no complaint with the two-year active duty docs. We were officers and doctors; they took us as they found us. Bukowski (corpsmen are only addressed by their last name, no first name and no rank, except if they are recruits, then they are addressed as seaman apprentice fucking recruit) was probably seaman first class, I forget, he was just Bukowski. He was always having too much liberty down in Greenwich Village on a weekend and the cops would call me to fish him out and get him back to base. Then he would have to face Captain's Mast and I would have to go with him to Captain (later Admiral) Yon, and assure the commandant it would never happen again "sir," "No," it would never happen again, sir." Sure.

Dirque, I know was a seaman apprentice fucking recruit because that's what Bukowski and Frankel would call him. He was an artist. I set him up with a studio in the same place where Rocco stayed at the end of the barracks. He also set up the loudest hi-fi music apparatus I ever heard playing music with which I was not familiar all day long, mostly Joan Baez recordings. I don't know how much work he did in the department. No chief of a department had ever set up an art studio for no seaman apprentice fucking recruit before out there to my knowledge.

Skarnellis (Barbara) always had a tale of woe, a crisis, a problem, and she would come to me. Years after I was separated from active duty she would call me in my office to talk. She married Paul, I didn't know his real name; he had been in a different department. And then she got cancer and I never heard from her anymore.

Frankel was of color. Not black African, but somewhat lighter, not exactly Caribbean either. There were no Dominicans at the base back then. I guess you would say he was light African American by today's definitions. Extremely intelligent, he was the boss of the group, probably seaman first class or petty officer of some rank, but not a chief.

They all adored me, maybe Frankel the most. He sensed something of unrest in me, very intuitive, I was going to start estrogen hormone shots to have a sex change even before I was finished my tour of active duty.

One time he said, "Dr. Raskind, you aren't very happy, are you?"

I only replied, "Why do you say that, Frankel?" No answer that I remember.

One day we were finished with the clinic, having coffee, and Frankel out of the blue says, "Dr. Raskind, let me show you some judo." He was an expert at judo, won some awards in the Navy for his prowess. The problem is there is a law, inviolate in the Navy, an enlisted man cannot touch an officer and vice versa. A sticky situation. He was willing to risk severe punishment, and cause some for me too, to show me some judo. I was not anxious to have my corpsman, lithe, wiry, a few years younger than I, unceremoniously, with damage to my dignity to say nothing of my back or the rest of me, flip me onto my back on the linoleum floor of the coffee mess. I understood my corpsmen very well, most of them quite happy to be the corpsmen, non-commissioned officers, with a leader like me.

Frankel, the smartest of the group, maybe looked up to me the most; he knew my skills as a doctor. He understood something of my unexpressed conflict. But there was more. He was the most aware of the chasm between corpsman and officer. It wasn't fair, for one moment he was going to undo that.

I said, "Okay, Frankel, what do you want me to do?" The other corpsman looked on in disbelief. My partner, Dr. Jansen, had gone home already, no one else in the clinic.

He said, "Grab my arm. Just grab my arm to attack me!"

So I did. Compliant, willing, obedient, the LCDR obeying the order of the noncom, the corpsman. I grabbed his arm, hard, tight. And very swiftly he grabbed my arm with both of his, applied the leverage of judo to flip me over his shoulder onto the floor. For a very long moment I felt myself ready to be catapulted over his shoulder, and then I suddenly realized there was no force on my arm at all. Frankel had released his grip, torn away from me and was holding his own shoulder with his other hand, in severe pain. He had dislocated it.

He had dislocated his shoulder once before, it re-dislocated. We took him to orthopedics, they reduced it. He didn't need surgery. We kept everything mum, nobody knew how it happened, maybe he was doing pushups. We had to fill out reports. He was alone when it happened.

I drove back to the city to my apartment across the street from the Manhattan Eye and Ear Hospital where I had trained two years before, my dog next to me in my '64 Corvette. I thought about Frankel, and I kept thinking about a play that had just become popular at that time. It was called *The Zoo Story*. I kept thinking about that play.

The Kid

The kids I grew up with—those who are still alive today—would have no trouble remembering who The Kid was, or is, in their mind's eye. Sometimes called The Thumper, or the Splinter or TW or Mister Wonderful, he was most often known as The Kid—and by the estimation of my generation certainly—as the greatest baseball batter who ever lived. Which of course was his own dream for himself, when he first came back east as a rookie and said, "All I want out of life is when I walk down the street folks will say: 'There goes the greatest hitter who ever lived.'" It was evident early on that he was destined for greatness, even by himself—for when he was introduced at spring training for the Boston Red Sox the first time, Hall of Fame manager Joe Cronin took him to meet the great Jimmie Foxx, who was the famous slugger for the team and a future Hall of Famer, and said, "Kid, wait until you see Jimmie Foxx hit."

Ted Williams replied, "Wait until Mr. Foxx sees me hit."

Statistics, in baseball more than all other major sports, define greatness. It is a game of stats. And by the stats Ted Williams may not have been the greatest hitter who ever lived. Babe Ruth hit more home runs; Ty Cobb had a higher lifetime batting average. Nonetheless, a combination of hitting for average plus power puts Ted Williams right up there with them. And then consider he lost four years of his prime when he was a Marine fighter pilot, one year from injuries, and refused to get easy base hits by not nullifying the Williams Shift that was employed because he would only pull the ball to right field where the infielders were positioned, leaving the whole left side of the diamond open for easy base hits. All that may well have given him the stats to be documented as what those of us who actually saw him play didn't need for corroboration—the greatest hitter of all time.

I didn't need the stats. I was a young baseball nut in the 1940s, and a NY Yankees fan besides. But when the Red Sox came to town to Yankee Stadium and I first saw Ted Williams, left-handed like me, tall, skinny, hit a home run that bounced into the Yankee bullpen between the bleachers and the right field stands in the old Yankee

Stadium he became forever my hero. That he was a loner—didn't tip his cap to the fans, marched to his own beat—was fine with me. I loved Joe DiMaggio, the Yankees star too, but Mr. Williams was special to me, as he was to adoring fans even outside Boston. When he batted for an average of .406 in 1941, I knew even then it was special. No one has hit .400 since.

Ted Williams has had plenty written about him over the years. In his heyday most of it from the press was negative—his unwillingness to patronize them, his frankness, his aloofness. But as he got older and people realized how warm and giving a person he was he became a hero to millions, and the acclaim of the two great players of their time in NY and Boston—Joe DiMaggio and Ted Williams— almost switched, Joe DiMaggio the aloof one, Ted Williams the generous one. And as affection for him grew long after he retired, so did stories about him. Everyone has a Ted Williams story. Here is mine.

I was on my way to Orlando, Florida, to go to a three-day golf school at Grand Cypress Academy, near Disney World, spring of 1985. I had been back practicing medicine in NYC since 1982 and after a few years I managed to build a country log home in Carmel, NY, where I now live full-time. Of course I had a tennis court in the backyard, but with few people to play with, and the beautiful golf course attached to the Sedgewood Club where my home was, I made a fateful decision to take up golf. And was forever hooked. The three-day course at Grand Cypress appealed to me. The latest in computer-generated golf swing teaching aids, video analysis, it was right up my alley. I was determined to learn a proper swing. Arleen and I flew to Orlando and then rented a car at the airport for the short trip to Grand Cypress, right outside Disney World. She would explore Epcot Center and Sea World while I worked on my swing. We were in the shuttle tram monorail car that shuffles between the exit area for our flight and the terminal a short distance away when I spied him.

No one in the world looks like Ted Williams except the great man himself. He was sitting at the end of the car, looking large even sitting down. There were only two bench seats, across the width of the car, one at each end, and he was at the far end one when we got on. I said to Arleen, "There is Ted Williams, wow," not sure if she knew what that meant. I told her. And I said, "Should I go over and say hello?"

I knew his reputation for aloofness, she didn't.

But she said, "Sure," and I walked over to him. I said, "Hi, Mr. Williams, don't want to bother you. I'm Renée Richards, just had to say hello. I saw you bounce plenty of those home runs into the Yankee bullpen at the stadium when I was a kid."

He looked up at me from the seat, and in his big booming voice, he said, "Sure, I know you, the tennis player, how are you?"—much to my relief. I had forgotten he played some tennis himself. In fact, he was known to have partnered his son John Henry in some doubles action on occasion. My friends who saw him play once had been amused that Ted would plant himself in the alley of the doubles court, expecting John Henry to cover the whole of the rest of it and shout, "Get that, John Henry. John Henry, get that" until it was pointed out that all the court except the doubles alley might be a little much for John Henry to cover. So at least he knew who I was. I said I was fine, I didn't want to bother him, but I just had to say hello. He then asked, "What are you doing in Orlando?" and I replied I was going to attend a short golf school at Grand Cypress. He then looked at me, paused for a moment and said, "Bet you have a good swing. What's your swing weight on the driver?"

Swing weight is a technical term to denote the specifications of a golf club relating to the weight of the club head to the shaft, like the old time scales in doctors' offices where one would move a weight along a scale until the weight balanced evenly with the weight of the person on the scale. I should not have been surprised by his question. Even though he was known as the greatest natural hitter of all time, those who really knew him knew what a perfectionist he was—how much attention to detail he paid—no matter what the endeavor. In World War II and in Korea he had to study physics and mathematics to learn the intricacies of piloting his fighter plane; he had barely had a high school education. John Glenn, the famous astronaut who had been a Marine fighter pilot first, said he would welcome Ted Williams as his wing man any day. And when his baseball career was finished, Ted had become an accomplished fly fisherman who knew all the intricacies of the world of fishing as well.

I was taken aback by the question, but I recovered to say, "I really don't know, I'm just getting acquainted with the game."

He thought a moment and then he blared, "D-4, I bet it's D-4." We chatted a few more minutes as the shuttle reached the terminal. I asked what he was doing in Orlando. I should have known. He said he was going fly fishing not far away. We shook hands and wished each other well and went on our way.

Three days at golf school, all very high-tech, and at the end each student was given a booklet documenting the necessary moves to a better swing, specifically for each student, based on the computer models generated from the videos taken. And at the end of the diagrams and suggestions there was written a list of all the golf clubs and the specifications recommended for each, for each student. I looked at the one for driver and there was written, "Driver—Swing weight D-4."

I was not surprised.

Wardrobe

Celebrated as one of this county's 100 greatest African Americans, Bill Cosby has been a comedian, actor, author, television producer, educator and activist. In the 1980s he produced and starred in the defining sitcom *The Cosby Show* on television. He also starred in the children's TV series *The Electric Company* and acted in several movies. In later life he became an activist and humanitarian. He was well-known for advising blacks to become responsible for their lives and to emphasize the importance of family. He has been the recipient of several honors and awards, including the Kennedy Center Honor, the Presidential Medal of Freedom, the Bob Hope Humanitarian Award and the Mark Twain Prize for American humor.

He was already a celebrity of great fame when I first met him at the Robert F. Kennedy Pro-Celebrity Tennis Tournament preceding the 1976 U.S. Open, then still held in Forest Hills, NY, at the West Side Tennis Club. I was just becoming notorious for my attempt to play in the U.S. Women's Open (it was not until the following year that I was granted permission by the court). Robert F. Kennedy (RFK) had been assassinated in 1968 and it was the leadership of his widow, Ethel Kennedy, who organized the yearly event at Forest Hills—still going on even now, the annual RFK Celebrity tournament. Mrs. Kennedy tried to reach me to invite me to participate, but I was hard to track down evidently. She sent me many messages. When I finally got one of course I called her right away, but she was out sailing off the Kennedy compound in Cape Cod near Hyannisport, Massachusetts, and we didn't connect until a day later.

When we finally spoke she said, "Renée, you are one tough lady to get a hold of."

I replied, "Mrs. Kennedy, you aren't so easy to reach either." I told her I would be delighted to play in the tournament.

The RFK Pro-Celebrity Tournament was a one-day round-robin doubles event followed by a huge dinner party in New York City—celebrities from the fields of entertainment, government and sports invited to participate. I had just become a celebrity of sorts in the public eye, but I was still basically an eye surgeon and tennis player. The doubles teams in the event paired a tennis pro with a celebrity. When I was paired as Bill Cosby's partner I assumed I was the tennis pro half of the duo although most of the other pros were in John McEnroe's class, not mine. Bill was the celebrity, although he had been an outstanding athlete in his younger days. We had much fun playing as a team, although I don't remember us winning a match. One of the teams we were matched, or overmatched, against was John McEnroe and basketball star Julius Erving of the Philadelphia Sixers NBA team. They were pretty hard to lob over as I remember. I also remember one shot from that match. I was serving, and Bill was at the net. My errant serve hit him right in the back of the head. He went down like a shot and we all rushed up to him to help. He was okay, nothing terribly wrong after getting banged on the noggin, but he lay on his back as if he were out cold, and I picked up on it, became my physician surgeon self, and put my ear to his chest to hear if his heart was beating, then began make believe chest massage to get his heart pumping again. We were a good comedy partnership and everyone in the stands laughed.

I remember the dinner well. First I met Muhammad Ali, who showed up at the cocktail party with his infant daughter in his arms, in a small room, it seemed, with more than a hundred guests smashed up against one another. At the dinner I was seated at the table with several Kennedy children, Caroline I remember, and some of the other Kennedy cousins. The Kennedys sure knew how to put on a party, and many dollars were raised for charity from the day's celebrations.

A few years after that RFK event I was living in Newport Beach, California, and one day Bill invited me to come to the TV show in which he starred, at the TV studio in Los Angeles, in front of a live audience. A few guests, like me, got to sit just off stage to watch the performance. I was thrilled to be there to see him in action. His show later became the number one TV show in America for five years running. When the live performance was over I was privileged to come backstage and visit while Bill hurriedly changed his shirt to get ready to fly to New York City for another engagement. In the middle of his preparations he looked around the room at his numerous assistants and asked, "Where's my T-shirt?" As he looked at each one the answer came, "I don't know." "I don't know." "I don't know." Finally, exasperated, late, tired, he put his hands on his hips, looked at the group around him, and said quizzically, "Who is in charge of wardrobe?"

I never forgot that. How pointed, how perfect a query and an answer could be. He didn't have to say: "I just put on a live performance of the best show on television of which I am the star. I am now getting ready to fly coast to coast to perform in New York City. I have a big and well-paid staff to help me. Do I have to take care of my wardrobe, my travel clothes, my T-shirt for the flight, too?" I never forgot it. "Who is in charge of wardrobe?" No anger, no malice, no admonishment. All he said was just "Who is in charge of wardrobe?"

Runner-up

Arleen and I took a trip a few years ago "down the shore"—or as it was said, "downa shaw" by the regulars who did it, for summer vacations or even just a weekend trip (like us). I did enough traveling by air when I was playing and coaching tennis around the world that I will be happy not to have to fly anywhere unless I have to anymore. It was September 2006 or maybe 2007, and we drove from New York City all the way down the shore to the southernmost point in New Jersey, to Cape May, where at the lighthouse at the tip you could see Delaware. A quaint town with little Victorian-style shops and larger homes, situated on the oceanfront, it has long been an attractive spot for vacationers to the beach along the Jersey Shore. Even a boardwalk, but no amusement park, there was one a little further north: Wildwood. The Garden State Parkway, running almost the full length of New Jersey, starts just north of Cape May and each mile is marked—the entrance to the Parkway from Cape May marked number 1. We arrived at an almost deserted town, like many along the shore. It was September, no more lifeguard at the beach, kids back at school, the rental houses vacant, few cars in town, and the shops and restaurants just right for us elder folks to browse, sit and enjoy in relative peace. Nothing like the beach after season.

We toured the lighthouse and a few historical sites, walked on the beach, and ate well in the restaurants; most of them open long after Labor Day. And as was inevitable after only a day I looked for a golf course. Cape May National, an old and venerated tract, welcomed visitors, and I made a tee time for that afternoon. It was just as I pictured, beautiful, unrestored, in good enough shape to enjoy, and with some challenging holes, carry over water, large areas of gorse brush and marsh between tee box and fairway. I signed up, no introductions, just assuming as I always do that nobody knows who I am, was given a cart, and I was off to play, alone, which was fine. I always enjoy playing with friends, and a foursome is better than two, but when I don't know anyone I usually prefer to be alone. To be paired with a nice stranger is okay, but a jerk could ruin the round.

I had played about five holes when I realized a golf cart always seemed to be near me, at a respectable distance behind—some thirty to forty yards—but there whenever I turned back to look. After a few more holes the golf cart was gaining on me, now only about twenty yards behind, close enough for me to see an old man wearing a Scottish golf cap sitting in the driver's seat. I also noticed a little white poodle running along slightly behind to the side of the cart.

Finally when I turned one more time and faced the man he shouted at me from about fifteen yards, "Did you ever play with Vines?" No hello, no excuse me, no introduction, just, "Did you ever play with Vines?" Of course I knew of Ellsworth Vines, Wimbledon champion, once number one tennis player in the world, reputed to have the best forehand ever, who retired from tennis to become a pro golfer (the only man ever to do so; the great Althea Gibson, winner of the ladies championship at Wimbledon and the U.S. Nationals the only woman).

I smiled at him and shouted back, "No, Vines won Wimbledon the year I was born." (1934) No further communication until I had teed off on the next hole.

The cart came close again and this time I heard, "Ever play Tilden?"

This time I laughed and said, "No, I only heard how great he was, before my time."

Bill Tilden of course is a legend in tennis, the greatest player of the first half of the last century, and a flawed hero for having been jailed for a time for homosexual behavior. I figured my new acquaintance would include Tilden in his curiosity about me, by now I had realized he knew of my notoriety. Probably assumed an association of me with any and all gender related persona.

Finally he came right alongside my cart, calling his little dog to jump on the bench next to him, "John Paul, John Paul, hop in," which he did. And then he said, "How about Bobby Riggs?" He had hit pay dirt. Bobby Riggs, Wimbledon champion in 1939 and more famous to the general public for losing to Billie Jean King in the Battle of the Sexes in the Houston Astrodome in 1973—which match according to Bobby put women on the map, was a good friend of mine. I played him several times, in friendly matches, and for money, even played as his partner for money in some not-too-friendly matches. He was—which was not common knowledge, and he liked it that way—a sensational golfer. He could win a lot of money hustling bets in golf. In tennis everyone knew how good he was.

I told my new acquaintance I had known Bobby, and well, but didn't go into details. And I won't just now. All I can say at this time is when he died and we were all gathered around the bedside crying for him and for ourselves that he would soon be gone, he said, "Don't feel sorry for me, I played golf and tennis my whole life. Don't feel sorry for me, I played golf and tennis my whole life." And he had.

There were no more questions. I got ready to tee off on the next hole, from the men's white tees. There was a carry over a long expanse of gorse requiring a drive of about 180 yards to reach the fairway.

As I got ready to tee off from the white tees, my new buddy yelled, "No, no, tee off from the reds (the ladies' tees farther forward) it's a long carry."

I said, "No, I'm okay, I can reach it."

I hit my drive, a good one fortunately, and then I noticed his cart parked ahead to the side, with him peering forward to the fairway, and he yelled, "Good, you made the fairway." He came alongside when I reached my ball and then said, "Hit it to the right; avoid that waste area on the left." I lined up my shot and of course I hit it into the waste area on the left. He yelled, "I won't bother you anymore," and off he drove.

I continued my round, enjoying the golf, my solitude, and wondering about my new friend. I didn't even know his name until I got to the last hole, in front of the 18th tee. There on a big rock was a bronze plaque with the face of a golfer with a Scottish cap on his head and inscribed below it, "This hole is dedicated to Skee Riegel, emeritus pro at Cape May National, who led the Masters for three rounds in 1951 and lost by two shots to Ben Hogan on the final day."

When I turned in my cart, the young head pro at Cape May said to me, "I see you met our old pro Skee on the course."

I said, "Yes, it was a pleasure, and thanks for the round."

Arleen picked me up and asked if I had had a good time. I told her I did, and all about Skee. I didn't go into the details of my thoughts about Skee. This is what came to mind: I won a few titles in my time. I lost in the finals of some too. No one remembers a finalist, a runner-up. Ben Hogan—a name even a casual golfer or sports fan might have heard. Ever hear of Skee Riegel? Leader in the clubhouse at the Masters for three rounds, lost to Ben Hogan by two shots in the final. A Masters champion, a changed life? The runner-up? Seemed pretty happy to me driving along the course with little John Paul at his side more than a half century later.

Notes from the world of golf:

*Riegel was nicknamed Skee by his childhood friends after they watched him take a pair of wooden planks off a barrel, tie them to the bottoms of his shoes, and ski down a hill near his suburban Philadelphia.

*From the Irish Golfer": Feb.25, 2009:

"One of the things I loved most about Skee was the way he always seemed to connect with anybody he came into contact with. It was just incredible. He always drew on something about the person, where they were from or where they went to school, and just made them feel special."

Riegel, a longtime Cape May resident, won the 1947 U.S. Amateur at Pebble Beach, Calif. He was also 4-0 in Walker Cup matches played at St. Andrews in Scotland (1947) and Winged Foot in New York (1949), respectively, and finished as low amateur at both the 1948 Masters and 1949 U.S. Open at Medinah in Illinois.

"In 1948, Skee was low amateur at the Masters and asked the officials if he got anything for it," said John Petronis, a former golf pro at Cape May National who first met Riegel in the 1990s. "They initially told him that he should be honored just to be there, but he pressed on and they eventually got an ash tray from Augusta National, engraved it for him, and presented it to him. That made Skee the first low amateur to actually bring something home from the Masters."

In 1951, a year after he turned professional, Riegel finished second to Ben Hogan at the Masters. Besides Hogan, Riegel also counted Bobby Jones, Byron Nelson and Sam Snead among his friends.

"I took Skee up to Winged Foot a few years ago for a ceremony and at the dinner that night he was supposed to meet with Arnold Palmer," Robert Mullock, president of Cape May National, said. "I took him over and Arnold introduced us to the president of Winged Foot. Skee looks over at the wall and sees a huge portrait of a golfer and asked the president who it is. The man told Skee, 'It's Bobby Jones.' Skee says, 'That's not Bobby Jones. I knew him for years and played golf with him and he looked nothing like that.' The president says, 'Of course he did. I painted that portrait myself.' "

Justice

My first experience with the court came in the 1960s when I was called to testify for a patient of mine who lost one eye when he was shot by a hunter in Long Island and sued for damages. I was a young ophthalmologist back then, still Richard Raskind, thirty-five years old, but I was already an associate professor of ophthalmology at Cornell Medical School, chief of the eye muscle service at Cornell and at the Manhattan Eye, Ear and Throat Hospital, and fast becoming an expert on binocular vision and depth perception, a good candidate to explain to a jury that two eyes are better than one. Losing one would deprive a person of significant visual function. The court was the NY State Supreme Court—in the county seat in Mieola, Nassau County, Long Island, and Chief Judge Sol Wachtler presiding. Judge Wachtler, also young for a judge, handsome, had great promise in judicial circles, even considered some day to become a judge in much higher chambers. Two young professionals of great potential brought together to help administer justice.

I tried to explain to the jury about three-dimensional depth perception, 3-D, which necessitated two eyes, the importance of a full field of vision, and the lifelong risk of blindness if an only remaining eye someday could not see. I wasn't persuasive enough; the jury came back with a verdict awarding what would be in today's world, a paltry sum—something like $10,000 for my patient. Judge Wachtler looked at me; I looked at him. We knew justice had not been done in the case. He knew I knew he knew it, and I knew he knew I knew it. We had nothing more to say. He thanked me for coming out from Manhattan to testify and I drove home. That he would later become imprisoned following a scandal of intense public interest involving an illicit love attachment that included stalking and blackmailing, and then never did rise to a high federal court let alone the supreme court he was once touted for…and that only five years later I would have a sex change and become even more notorious than he had nothing to do with justice that day in Mineola.

I had a better experience in court some years later. By then I was Dr. Renée Richards, still an expert on binocular vision, double vision, and all that. This time I was called to Workmen's Compensation Court in Brooklyn. A patient had suffered an injury on the job to the eye muscles of one eye, resulting in restricted eye movements and double vision in straight ahead gaze and when he looked up. He could only see single when he would tip his chin up and look down. Two-thirds of his visual field was compromised, not useful. The judge was a woman, still not common then in the early 1980s, but that did not give me any cause for apprehension. What did, however, was that she looked like a floozy, sitting there with her black robe over her dress, high heels showing under the table where she sat, long blond hair down to her shoulders, lots of eye makeup and caked face foundation, sitting there painting her long fingernails bright red as she listened to the proceedings. I was not encouraged. I wasn't even sure she heard any of my discourse. Nonetheless, when I finished explaining the patient could only use his eyes without seeing double in the lower third of his total field of vision, I was not at all sure I had made any progress in my elaboration of this clinical condition.

The judge abruptly looked up from her fingernails and said, "Okay, two-thirds out, only useful in one third, 66 percent disability awarded," and banged her gavel on the desk. "Next case." Then she turned to me and said, "Dr. Richards, for your appearance, $500. Thank you for coming to Brooklyn." Of course, she had got it exactly right—you can't tell the book by its cover.

My next recollection of justice had nothing to do with me. It was just such an appalling miscarriage of justice I have to mention it here as prelude to my own participation in injustice, which had happened a few years earlier. It was the O.J. Simpson trial and verdict—the case of the football star who was acquitted of killing his wife and her friend in Los Angeles, perhaps the most notorious miscarriage of justice at the time, even for decades. I was playing golf with my dearly departed friend Alan King, the famous raconteur and comedian, at his club Fresh Meadow in Long Island. Same club, by the way, where the infamous Bernie Madoff scammed several of his close friends out of millions some years later, talk about justice. I was playing with Alan and two close friends of ours when we finished the first nine holes, and ran to the clubhouse in time to hear the verdict on TV. "Not guilty." It was astonishing, to us, to the whole country (and of course in a later civil suit O.J. was found guilty, but not sent to jail).

Alan King was a staunch supporter of justice, a believer in our system of justice, besides being a liberal and a proud supporter of President John F. Kennedy. He had a room at his home in Kings Point—the Kennedy Room—with many souvenirs of his meeting the Kennedys, photographs, and other mementos. Moreover he was a defender of our way of life, our constitution, especially our court system. He was also, in fact, and totally unrelated to this story, the friend who advised me about seeking the best lawyer to plead my case when I sued the tennis associations for the right to play at the U.S. Open. We ran in to the bar where the TV set was suspended above and watched. The verdict was announced. "Not guilty." Alan could not believe it, nor could my friends Steve Levy and Larry Parsont, nor me. Alan became so upset he said a quick goodbye to us and went right home. He did not play the back nine with us. His belief in justice had been badly shaken. I dared not think of telling him, nor my two good friends, the story of my own participation in injustice. But I will now.

In 1981, I was living in Gainesville, Florida. It was my home in between traveling to tennis tournaments where I was either playing or coaching Martina Navratilova. Much to my surprise I received in the mail one day a call to jury duty; to my surprise because as a practicing physician I had never ever been called before. Doctors just did not get called to jury duty. At this interval of my life, however, I was not practicing medicine, and the local board of jurors in Alachua County decided to call me, like everyone else, to appear for jury duty. So I went. I had not the slightest doubt that, since at that time I was still a pretty notorious and controversial public figure, I would be sent home. Wrong. Not in Gainesville, Alachua County, North Central Florida. In fact, not only was I called, I was picked for a jury and told to come back on Friday for the trial.

When I appeared on Friday at the appointed time, noon, I was ushered in to the courtroom with the five other jurors (six make up a jury for the cases like this one in Florida). I learned it was a case of a woman who had been arraigned by the court after being picked up by the state police on suspicion of drunk driving. The woman sat in the defendant's box. Guilty as charged. At least by me. If there ever was a chronic alcoholic sitting in front of me here she was. About fifty years old, looking quite a bit older, no makeup, unkempt straggly gray hair, sallow face, pale, heavily lined, little expression. I had seen that face many times when I worked in the free clinic at the Eye Hospital in New York City. And maybe I had seen her sitting at a bar a few times, face resting on her arm on the bar, nursing one whiskey after another, or perhaps someone who looked just like her. I didn't need a trial to convince me. But here I was, a juror, so I had to pay attention, give her the benefit of the doubt, and not jump to conclusions before the evidence, as is said.

I learned she had a record, three times previously arrested for drunk driving, no time served. The state police officer who filed the complaint was called to testify. He strode in and took his seat in the witness chair, one leather jackbooted leg swung over the other, legs spread apart, with one knee sticking out to one side. He looked at the crowd in the courtroom and winked. The courtroom was silent. He was hated on sight. He proceeded to tell how he had seen the defendant weaving across the road, and when he caught up to her and got her stopped, he opened the door on the driver's side and she fell out onto the pavement. There was no sobriety test, no breathalyzer, no need for either—she was put in the back of the police cruiser, no handcuffs needed, and deposited in the city jail. The only witness was his partner, who didn't look much different than he did, smart uniform, jack leather boots, Canadian Mounted Police type, broadbrimmed hat in his lap. I did not realize it at the time, they looked like good old boys as was said in those parts; you know, North Central Florida in the last century.

I don't remember much in the way of other details of the trial except the woman protested, "I wasn't drunk. I didn't even drink one." One what I was not sure, but I had some idea, and also that it wasn't just one. After a few hours it was over, there were no other witnesses, and the jurors filed into the adjacent room for deliberations. First order of business was to select a foreman to run the proceedings. As surprised as I was I had been selected for a jury in the first place, nothing compared to suddenly realizing I had been chosen to be the foreman. (Or forewoman in my case, excuse me.) After

111

getting over that shock, I started the discussion by going around the room and asking each juror what his or her thoughts, feelings, opinions, convictions were. The first juror I asked said, "She is not guilty." I was dumbstruck, but I kept my peace. Second juror: "Not guilty." Third juror: "Not guilty." Each and every one simply: "Not guilty." I had thought I would get a discussion started by asking each one to say something, ask a question, or talk about the evidence. But no, all I got was a unanimity of opinion that this repeatedly, chronically, miserable, obviously alcohol-addicted sister of the county was not guilty of driving under the influence of alcohol, weaving and swerving all over the road, and falling out of the car onto the ground when the state trooper opened her door. Unanimous so far, five out of six. It did not take me long to realize that of the six jurors I was the only one not of like mind and also the only one not a born and bred North Floridian from Gainesville. And it took not much longer for me to realize what my options were.

It was approaching five o'clock. The afternoon sun was streaming in the window of the jury room. If I were to start reasoning with this jury, presenting them with evidence that to me seemed so obvious not even to have to be repeated, that this poor lady was guilty as sin, it was going to take me a long time into the evening, if indeed possible at all. And, to my discredit, although I would probably do the same thing all over again if so presented with the situation—I checked the time and understood quickly that if I were to start my arguments I would miss the phone call to New York City with my son. Every Friday it had been arranged that Nicky and I would get to talk to each other—no matter where in the world I was at the time—promptly at 6 p.m. Eastern Standard Time. Nothing was going to keep me from that date, that reunion, by telephone, with my eight-year-old son, nothing.

I looked around the room. The jurors looked at me, waiting for my opinion. And when I looked at them I realized something else, beside my expectant phone call to Nicky. I realized—these people, the other jurors, these citizens of the town in which I was living but had not been born, had such a hatred of the police that almost no crime of one of its fellow citizens could lead to a conviction—except perhaps murder or rape. This poor woman versus the Florida State Police—no contest. I turned to them and said, "Well, I guess its unanimous, let's go home." We walked in to the courtroom, and the judge asked me if we had reached a verdict. I said, "Yes, your honor, not guilty."

And just as had been the case in Nassau County, Long Island, New York, when Chief Judge Sol Wachtler of the NY State Supreme Court locked eyes with the young eye surgeon from New York City, Richard Raskind, so too, fifteen years later, the Alachua County Chief Judge, Gainesville, Florida, looked at Renée Richards, tennis player, tennis coach, recent citizen of the county—and she looked at him—and they each knew the other knew justice had not been served.

Rastaman

There is a distinction between runaway and missing. The police officer from the 19th Precinct—East Side, Midtown Manhattan—which included my office at 40 Park Avenue, explained that to me after I reported my thirteen-year-old son had not been heard from since he had left his grandfather's house in Forest Hills, in Queens, where he had been living temporarily. Missing means foul play is suspected. Runaway, I was told, applied to Nicholas—he had just run away. Just like that.

I should not have been surprised. Nothing he ever did was surprising, but running away had not been one of his ventures. The note he had left on his grandfather's hall table said, "Grandpaw, went to the city. Be back later, love, Nick." Yes, that's the way he wrote grandpa—like he spelled in general, phonetically, like the word sounded—like "allso" for "also." He was a talented writer, his sixth grade teacher at St. Bernard's School had said so, but spelling was not his forte. Despite the Temple Emanu-El Nursery School, the Episcopal School, St. Bernard's, The Walden School, two summer sessions first at Taft and then at St. George's (two of the preeminent prep schools in the Northeast), the Fay School in Massachusetts, Intermediate School No. 14, in Corona, Queens, and Bill's private tutoring school in Manhattan—that is how he spelled—neither his mother nor I ever having supervised his homework.

He attended the Temple Emanu-El nursery school because his nanny, an old Colombian woman named Mia (Maria) had heard from the other, fancy Irish white, nannies in Central Park that it was the best, and we lived right across 66th Street from the entrance. On her own she took Nick there when he was two-and-a-half.

The officious director looked down at this old Indian woman and asked, "What is this little boy's name?"

And a voice came up from almost under her desk, "My name is Nicky Raskind."

And then, "Where does this little boy live?" and the little voice replied, "Twenty-one East 66th Street."

Finally, "How old is this little boy?"

And from below, "I am two-and-a-half years old."

The director turned to Mia, "He can start on Monday."

Three good years there, punctuated by having three of his parents in attendance for the first Passover Seder for his class. One parent was supposed to be there for each student. His mother thought his father wouldn't come because he was operating in the hospital, his father thought that since his mother was gentile she would probably forget, and his grandfather thought neither parent would come so he made sure to drive in from Forest Hills to be there. And so little Nicky had three parents in attendance to help recite the Haggadah.

When he graduated from nursery school his mother put him in the Episcopal School, and after his first day there I asked him what he had learned. He put his hands above his head and yelled, "Heaven above," then his hands brought down to his feet, he shouted, "Hell below. Joshua fit the battle of Jericho." It was also a wonderful school too and a good prep for the rigors of St. Bernard's, where he attended happily until the seventh grade. Then began the series of school experiences culminating—or at least contributing to—his running away. Not the least of which, although I don't like to think about it, the revelation of my sex change having been made known to a few of his classmates.

He had not come back from the city, and when I reported that to his mother the next morning I was given the usual commandment, "Do something." This time I had no idea what. He was not at his best friend Alex's apartment, and none of his other friends had heard from him either. Moreover, it was beyond my imagination he could have run away. I really should not have been surprised. I had told him he was not going to stay permanently with Grandpa; in fact, he was to be sent to live with my sister in Oregon, on her farm, an onerous and ominous threat it evidently had been. He knew my sister, had in fact spent a week with her and his three cousins at their home. He liked them and the horses, but to have to stay under her roof and jurisdiction, no way. He had his own ideas about her influence on me as a child.

I had been at my wit's end. Staying with Grandpa was hardly satisfactory. He almost never went to the junior high school where he was enrolled near there. It was a far cry from the Fay School and most certainly not like St. Bernard's—the other kids, mostly from Corona, Queens (just beyond the border for upper-middle-class Forest Hills) harboring knives or other weapons sneaked thru the metal barriers at the school entrance—also his schoolmates not exactly like his old classmates from private prep school. The truant officer called me daily in my office on Park Avenue in Manhattan to ask where my son was, and me forever replying, "I am sure he is at school." And almost every night Nick would call me to say a burglar was lurking in the backyard and I better drive out there from the city and stay overnight, which I frequently did. The stay at Grandpa's was supposed to be his punishment, not mine. Especially after his mother had found evidence of smoking paraphanalia—pipes and bongs and such—in his room in her house in Southampton.

After that brief spring term at public junior high school I had let him stay with my friend, then bachelor, Michael Stone—Man of Stone we called him—at his house in Southampton for the summer, another of my many mistakes I do admit. It was a liberal education for a fourteen-year-old to say the least. Not surprising that Nick had told me, "You ruined my summer," when I picked him up there in August and said, "That's it." No more bachelor life to observe, partake, enjoy—ruining his summer indeed.

For whatever reason, or combination thereof—"no party life in Southampton," time to get serious for a fall term at school, threat of being sent to Oregon, caught smoking—he decided to split, to run away. He did just that. It took me a few days to realize and accept he had truly done that to me.

At St. Bernard's School, the sons of waspy, wealthy and influential New Yorkers were groomed to go on to the elite prep schools of the Northeast and then to Harvard or Yale or other prestigious institutions of higher education, after which they would take their place as leaders of government and industry as it was said. When I was asked to report to the headmaster with Nick early in the term that would have been his seventh grade there, he had been there three years, doing well. I knew it was not going to be positive. I went in first, and tried to be convincing to the Episcopalian minister who was the headmaster that my son was about to knuckle down and get serious about his studies, to fulfill the promise he had shown only the year before. I did my best, but when Nick went in after me and came out within three minutes I knew his career at St.Bernard's was over.

I asked him, "What happened?"

He replied, "He asked me what I wanted to be when I grew up and I said 'I want to be a drug dealer in Thailand.'"

He was then sent to the Fay School, a boarding school in Massachusetts, co-ed, not rigid, a warm and non-competitive environment, and he actually liked it for a time. But soon after I sent the tuition for the second term, and after sending up the hi-fi set and the hockey equipment and the new desk set for his room, I got an emergency call from the headmaster. "Dr. Richards, you better come up and get your son, he is threatening to tear the school apart." I had Nick put on an airplane to La Guardia Field in Queens, in New York City. He was met by his mother and his father (yes, me) at the airport. For both of us to be there together, at the same time, gave testimony to the gravity of the situation. From the airport it was only a five-minute drive to Grandpa's house in Forest Hills, where Nick was deposited to stay. Until the summer in Southampton, and then until after which he became a runaway.

I had heard about children running away, or worse, missing. I saw the movie *Missing,* which dramatized one family's anguish when it happened to them. And I had no idea my son was only a runaway and not missing. He had been told "don't take the subway," at night from the city to Forest Hills, and "don't ride with strangers,"—he knew all that, he was a very savvy kid growing up in New York City, having experienced more than most for his age to be sure. When he was not heard from the day after he left the note to his Grandpa, and when all the phone calls to friends were a dead end, I had to face it—my son was missing or a runaway—it didn't make any difference to me. I reported the details to the police officer from the 19ᵗʰ Preceinct. I told my next-door neighbor in the country, Jim Dunn, retired NYC detective who had his own private investigation firm after he left the police force. Jim said he would start an investigation. He was not reassuring. He did not allay any of the fears I was beginning to feel, foul play the most paramount.

And that is why I started my own investigation. I kept in touch with Nick's two best friends, who were at school in the city. They had not seen him. I told them to keep asking friends for leads. Frustrating work, I was given a few misleading false sightings. One boy said Nick had been sighted on Park Avenue in the 80s on a bike. I didn't believe it. He was into skateboards, not bikes. But the boy swore he had seen him. I began to search Manhattan myself. Every day that week after office hours I would walk up and down the vast sheep meadow in Central Park, where Nick and I had spent so many afternoons when he was little. What a sight, this tall, broad shouldered, I might say, maybe scary, woman accompanied by her large Airedale Terrier, JP, a handful, or armful, to control, stopping every teenager who walked by and shoving Nick's picture in his face. No one recognized it. Or admitted it. Maybe they thought I was an undercover cop. And when I exhausted Central Park I started in on Washington Square Park in Greenwich Village. The same thing—"Have you seen my son? Do you recognize this picture?"—to no avail. Washington Square Park was home to junkies, dealers, crack addicts, heroin, marijuana, buyers and sellers. A busy place. I interrogated anyone and everyone, especially anyone who looked Jamaican.

I knew Nick's love of anything Jamaican—reggae music and Bob Marley's picture larger than life in his room in the city and at Grandpa's. The Jamaicans in the park drew a blank. I described him: Five-foot-six, hair short on the side, longer on top, dark eyes, dark hair, earring with a cross in his left ear, baggy grey torn canvas pants, torn sneakers, T-shirt emblazoned with a rock group on the front, skateboard under his arm. I didn't add handsome. It was obvious from the picture I shoved in their faces. Why couldn't they recognize it? And why couldn't I realize every kid I sighted from behind who was surely my son was surely not when I got up close to see his turned face. Some of the junkies just looked up at me with a blank face from their squat on the grass by the walkway, or answered me with a plea for a few pennies. The chess players were annoyed when I interrupted their games—"Have you seen my son?" and thrust his picture between their faces and the chessboard.

When I went to the skateboard shop uptown and showed Nick's picture to the owner he told me he looked familiar.

"Did you sell him a bike?"

The boy who worked there said, "He was into skateboards, not bikes."

I was losing my patience. "I know he was into skateboards, he might have bought a bike," I blurted.

Every lead a dead end, and each evening after canvassing Washington Square I would call Barbara and Grandpa and report, "Nothing." Every lead a dead end.

He had now been missing five days. Five days of anguished trekking in the parks, calling everyone I could think of, all fruitless. And then it came to me. I finally realized he was not seen at any of the places I searched because he was in Jamaica. How he got there by himself a mystery—no money, no passport, it seemed impossible—but I became convinced that indeed, of course, that was where he was. I had been given some clues during the week. Man of Stone said a young woman who was a friend, who had known Nick from the summer in Southampton, had said he had told her he was going to Jamaica. Mimi, the mother of Nick's close friend Alex, said so too. And then, the clincher—I called the Fay School where Nick's close friend Tom was still attending. I convinced the headmaster to threaten Tom with expulsion if he didn't disclose where Nick might be.

Under duress he said, "Jamaica." It all fit. His hero, Bob Marley, the music, the pot, how could I have missed all that?

119

And then Barbara called. She exclaimed, "He's in Jamaica." A friend of hers called from London and told her Nick had disclosed to her that if he ran away it would be to Jamaica. I had heard enough.

Arleen was not happy when I told her to get me a ticket to Jamaica. I stick out in a crowd, at home in New York City, anywhere. In Jamaica I would certainly not go unnoticed. I did not care. My mind was made up.

I called my dear friend, ex-Wimbledon champion Dick Savitt, who had spent many winters at the Racquet Club in Montego Bay. "Dick, where would a kid go to run away in Jamaica?"

"Negril Beach, but be careful," he said.

I stopped at Grandpa's house in Forest Hills on the way to the airport at LaGuardia. I checked Nick's room, my old room when I was a child—a picture of me at age 17 by his bed, the floor covered with clothes and skis and boots and books and tapes and Coke bottles—nothing to suggest where in Jamaica he might have gone. The Jamaican flag on the wall, and Bob Marley's picture confirmed the country, but no clue beyond that.

Arriving in Montego Bay after a stop in Miami, it was already 9 p.m. when I stood at the immigration desk Friday night and filled out the landing form—including destination in Jamaica. I was told my destination was too vague; I had to name a hotel. I looked at the list provided for Montego Bay hotels, even though I knew I would only be there overnight. Negril is a two-hour ride along the coast from there. Doctor's Cave hotel seemed appropriate enough. I wrote it down as my destination. It was not far from the airport and I thought if I had to check arrival forms from New York earlier in the week I could get back there in the morning to do that.

When I checked in to Doctor's Cave, Jump, the young Jamaican who took my overnight case up to the room for me, asked, "How are you doing? I hope you have a good stay in Jamaica." I allowed I was not doing so hot and I was there, not for a vacation, but for a reason, to find my son. I showed him Nick's picture and asked where he thought a teenager like that might hang out. He volunteered that after work he would ask around at some of the discos he knew—if anyone as young as Nick had been there during the week. But he would not get off work until 1 a.m.

Once in my room I called Lady Sarah Churchill—yes, the daughter of the famous wartime Prime Minister of England, Winston Churchill, another amazing piece to this saga. Sarah Churchill lived in Redding, Jamaica, not far from Montego Bay. She happened to be the grandmother of Nick's closest friend Alex. I knew Alex's mother Mimi, Lady Churchill's daughter. Lady Sarah, as she was known in Jamaica, knew everybody of any importance on the island, as one could imagine. She was willing to call the head of immigration in Montego Bay and have him check the entries for that week. She reported back to me—No one named Nick Raskind or Nick Isles (Barbara's married name) had entered Montego Bay from Monday through Friday. The immigration chief had checked every flight.

I was still not to be put off. I knew he was there, somewhere, however he had managed it. I tried to get some sleep. Tossing and turning a few hours with no luck I went back to the airport to the immigration office, alone. It was a vast room with many desks; empty at that hour—6 a.m.—except for one man and one woman sitting at their desks, guarding the entrance. When I told them I wanted to go thru every entry from to Montego Bay from Monday thru Friday from New York City they were aghast. They explained, "You can't do that." Besides, there were many flights, three different airlines, some coming via Miami, some from New York direct. It couldn't be done even if they allowed me to look. And then they realized I was not going away. So, the three of us sat there as the Jamaican sun came up outside the window, going over each and every entrance slip looking for a Nick Raskind or a Nick Isles.

When we finished, with no success, the woman turned to me and said evenly, "Go home, your son is not on the island."

Arleen had said, "Don't go to Jamaica, it's a wild goose chase."

When I got back to the hotel, I sat out in front of its wall by the curb, motionless, distraught, depressed, but no more deterred from my

121

mission. I would find him. I sat there until my new friend Jump came back from checking the discos.

I yelled, "Jump, we have to go to Negril. Where is it?"

He replied, "It's down the coast, a two-hour drive." He had no car, but he would ask his friend Johnson who had a minivan to drive us. And when Johnson arrived later in the morning off we went. I sat in the front, next to Johnson. Jump sat in the back. Along the way we stopped at two hotels, showed Nick's picture around, no luck, and on we went. I checked into The Sundowner, a small hotel at the edge of Negril and left my overnight bag there. I had no idea how long I would be there. As long as it would take, I knew that. Negril Beach until only a few years before had been a tiny beach town, often popular with honeymooners. Tourists who stayed there he would be given a lantern to find their way to their cottage in the evening—no running water, no telephone, no electricity. In recent years it had grown to become *the* place for young people to hang out, or to escape from the serious world in the States. Marijuana, cocaine everywhere, and anything could happen in Negril. Far worse, just north of the beach in the hills above, where the drugs were grown—murder, kidnapping, and even the local police did not venture there. At this time, in the fall, summer vacation in the States was over, but there was still a small group of young American kids to be seen motor biking down the road or walking on the beach.

I had no idea where to start looking, but Barbara had given me the name of a friend, English, who had a home on the beach—Seagate it was called—and I thought I might just as well start there. The friend who lived there I was told might not be on the island, but his caretaker would be. Jump and Johnson drove me straight there. There was a locked iron gate with a sign above it, Seagate, and a sign on the side of the gate read, Bad Dog.

We rang the bell and Elijah, the caretaker, came to greet me. I told him Barbara knew his boss. I showed him Nick's picture. Soft spoken, slight, quiet, gentle, he looked at it and said simply, "If he is in Negril we will find him."

We drove off down the road parallel to the beach, the only paved road in the town. We saw a few other roads, non-paved, that pointed toward the hills to the north. That would be our next destination if the beach did not prove fruitful. But no one relished going up in the hills. A little jeep with *Police* written on the hood, and a blue light on the top came by from the opposite direction. We hopped out of the van and gave the policeman a description of Nick, and showed him his picture. Another amazing happening. The policeman said he already had a description of Nick—given to him by a detective in New York. It must have been my old next-door neighbor Jim Dunn investigating for me from New York. We gave him a picture of Nick and he said he would keep looking. He reiterated what we already knew, "Don't go up in the hills." Not even the police go up there.

We drove on along the beach, past some cabins with a sign out in front, Ozzie's Shack. I was filled with anxiety, exhausted, but somehow innervated by what was taking place—Jump, and Johnson, the local police, the small size of the town—all in spite of having been told "go home, your son is not on the island." And then, almost like a dream, I saw him. All those times in the parks in New York City, all those times on Park Avenue, all those times up close not him, false alarms. This time, thirty yards in front of me, walking toward our van, was my son. Wearing shorts and a T-shirt, barefoot, a Jamaican youth walking beside him.

I yelled to Jump and Johnson, "There he is." And pointed to Nick. I was in a state of shock.

But nothing I can imagine to that of my son when I put my head out of the van and shouted, "Nick, it's me, get in the van."

He had escaped from my world, had gone into his own, had been there a week—and suddenly with no warning, I exploded his haven. And then he said, "I'm not coming with you," as I grabbed his arm and he pulled away.

"Get him," I yelled as the three of us jumped out of the van. Nick was well behind the van when Jump and Johnson caught up with him. I repeated, "Get in the van." I was shaking, my whole body was shaking. A scuffle ensued as I said, "You come with me or you go with the police." And we got him in the back of the van. He was crying and screaming that I had no business being there, it was his place, he didn't want me there, I had no business being there, and then he hit my arm. He actually hit my arm.

Jump and Johnson tried to calm him. "Take it easy, mon, take it easy." In their own laid-back Jamaican way they were marvelous with him, lots better than me.

We drove back to Seagate. As I got out of the car to report to Elijah that Nick was found, to call off the search, I heard Nick yelling to Jump and Johnson from the van, "Do you know who that is? That person is my father." And he kept shouting, "That's my father. That's my father."

I went back to the back of the van. "Nick, say hello to Elijah, he is a friend of Barbara's." He was in no mood to say hello to anybody.

When Elijah looked at him he said, "Do you think you will need any help getting him back to the airport?"

I agreed, "Yes, I think I will." We arranged for Elijah to meet us at my hotel, the Sundowner, where I would go to pick up my suitcase. He said Constable Francis would meet us there too, in streetclothes, to help us to the airport.

When we got to the Sundowner Nick had calmed down a little, me not so much. I said, "Let's go in and have a drink." When we sat down at a table, under a grapevine overhead, the beach and the ocean beyond, I asked him if he wanted to eat and he replied he only ate in the evening, like the Rastafarians. He would have a beer. I was in no state to say no and we both had a Jamaican beer. Loosening up he said he was a Rastafarian, I was ruining his life, and he wanted to stay in Jamaica. At that point Jump and Johnson, who had sat down with us, got up and moved to another table. How lucky had I been to have found them. They seemed to know exactly what to do every step of the way. Nick thought they were Jamaican secret police, that I had arranged that. I thought they were extraordinary adolescent psychologists—of course they were neither.

We both loosened up. Constable Francis arrived, not in uniform. I thanked him and said, "I don't think I need a police escort to the airport, thank you." We drank our beer and talked. And I asked him if he would come back with me if he could live with Alex in the city. I said he didn't have to live with Barbara or me, and certainly not my sister Josephine, and he could choose any school he wanted, except the last one he attended which was filled with kids with issues worse, even, than his. He agreed to living with Alex and his mother Mimi, and agreed we would find another school. I collected my suitcase, and then on to Ozzie's Shack, where it turned out was where he had been staying. He picked up his knapsack and said goodbye to his friend who had been walking with him on the beach.

The owner came out, an elderly Jamaican man. "He's a good boy," he said. "He was going up into the hills. We told him not to. I told him he should go home. We call him Rastaman. I told him, 'Go home, Rastaman.'" I thanked him.

As if the whole saga were not unbelievable enough as it was, we stopped in Redding at Lady Churchill's home to report to her that he was found. She came out, and yelled, "Don't get out of the van." Her Jack Russell Terriers, four of them, were growling around the van, waiting to nip the heels of anyone getting out. She peered in the window and said, "Any luck?"

I pointed in the back and replied, "There he is."

She looked at him and said, "Nick, would you like to stay with me for a while and cool off?" She could see he had calmed down but was still not exactly docile.

I interrupted, "No, he is coming with me. Thank you. He is coming with me."

Then, spontaneously, she said, "Would you like to live with my grandson Alex? My daughter has offered for you to stay with them."

Unrehearsed, she had suggested what I had proffered an hour before. He agreed to do that.

At the airport Jump and Johnson said goodbye. Maybe someday Nick would see them again in Jamaica. He knew he would return. And then, as if he had just been on a school vacation with me like we had done many times, he says he wants to buy T-shirts and souvenirs. I was dumbstruck as I forked over a few dollars for T-shirts. Wanted by the police in two countries, he buys T-shirts. And then before we boarded our flight, damned if the same two immigration officers from when I had arrived weren't sitting there at their posts as we came through. The woman looked at me, then at Nick. She said nothing about his having sneaked into Jamaica; to this day I still don't know how he did it.

She just turned to me and said evenly, "I see you found your son," and then to Nick, "Why do you give your mother such a hard time?"

He did not correct her as to which parent I was. He simply said, "Because she gives me a hard time." And we boarded our flight.

We had plenty of room, only a few passengers on board, so we sat in a row of three seats, the middle one empty, better that way, and talked. He said how it was just chance I had found him, that he almost never just walked along that road. I said it made no difference. I would have found him anyway. I wasn't leaving Negril until I did.

Grandpa came down the stairs of the house in Forest Hills to see Nick standing there with his knapsack on his back. When I had asked him on the airplane how he could have done such a thing as run away to all the people who loved him he had said he didn't care—the only ones he was unhappy about were his Grandpa and his little brother Philip. Nonetheless I called his mother. She knew I would find him.

I ran away once too. So did his mother. Not exactly the way he did, however. I told him on the airplane he should never do that again— because he knows I have a tachycardia condition and I had had three tachycardia attacks during the past week.

126

He said, "Well, don't do what you did to me again and you won't get anymore tachycardia attacks."

He does still like Jamaica. He went with Grandpa for a school spring break a year later. I watched them walking down the ramp to get into the airplane, yelling at each other, and when I came to pick them up three days later I saw them yelling at each other as they came up the ramp off the plane.

"Did you have a good time?" I asked when they reached me.

"Yeah, it was great. Grandpa went in the water every day."

And the following year Nick and I went there again, on spring break—the hotel we were to stay at in Montego Bay was crowded and not really authentic Jamaica. We didn't even check in, we got in our rental car and drove down the coast. We found a more relaxed, more informal place on the beach, in a town called Runaway Bay.

I swear it.

He Put Women on the Map

In 1939 Bobby Riggs won the Gentlemen's Singles championship at the All England Lawn Tennis and Croquet Club, as it was known then (Wimbledon as we know it now). It was in the days before Open Tennis—there was no prize money, just a big ornate trophy to the winner. Bobby had bet as much money as he could with the bookies in London on himself to win. He took his winnings and bet them all on the men's doubles final, which he and his partner, Elwood Cooke, won, and then he took the combined winnings from the singles and the doubles and bet it all on Alice Marble and himself to win the mixed double, which they did. He would have come home on the boat from Southampton, England, with $105,000, but because of World War II the money was held in England. When he finally collected in 1945 it had gained considerable interest.

Despite that remarkable triple, as well as hundreds of other titles, including being ranked number one in the United States at every age group in which he ever competed—from junior days to seniors and even super seniors in his 70s, despite being the number one player in the world as an amateur (1939) and then as a professional (1946, '47), he is known in the public for basically one match—the Battle of the Sexes against women's champion Billie Jean King in the Astrodome 1973—seen by millions on TV and won by Billie Jean 6-4, 6-3, 6-3. Forever after he was known as the loser of that match and whenever queried about it his answer was always the same, and not a bit reflecting the true disappointment he felt at the loss—"I put women on the map." In a way, ironically, in the struggle at the time for women's rights, including women's pro tennis, he did. He was also wrongly labeled a sexist, the fact is he was not, he had been taught tennis by a woman tennis coach in Los Angeles as a junior, had great respect for women of accomplishment, and on his deathbed Billie Jean, a spearhead of the Women's Movement, called him to say, "I love you."

Besides being a great tennis player he was also a gambler and an inveterate hustler. He would bet on anything—tennis, golf, cards, backgammon, and almost always would win. Especially crafty with the golf—he could get bets that were favorable because hardly anyone knew how great a golfer he was. In tennis prospective suckers were harder to find, those in the know knew how good he was in a money match and how good a psychologist he was in gaining the best wager for himself. I remember one friend of mine on whom Bobby played his mind games like a shrewd psychiatrist, forever playing upon his ego, and underlying feeling of inferiority, to extract a bet. One time I won a practice match (Bobby's euphemistic phrase for a money match) from him at the old Great Neck Country Club where we were both members. I showed my winnings—a ten dollar bill–to pro John Nogrady, who said immediately, "Frame it." Money wins over Bobby were rare.

I first met Bobby at that club in Great Neck, hardly a country club, just a row of dirt clay courts along the railroad track near the train station in Great Neck, Long Island. Many of the top players in the New York metropolitan area played there. Bobby lived in nearby Plandome on the north shore of Long Island. Every spring, one of the first to drive by, he would yell down to the courts from the road above, "Hey, Doc, how are you doing? You look pretty good, how about a practice match?" Bobby didn't play anything unless it was for money. Why bother?

One time one of the old pros in Great Neck got so mad at losing to Bobby–in everything—he decided he would practice something Bobby didn't do and then challenge him to a bet. So he took cardboard beer coasters—the round flat cardboards that used to be served at the bar under a bottle or glass of beer—and he practiced throwing them up against a wall to see how close he could get the coaster to the wall without hitting it. When he got good at it he invited Bobby for a drink at a bar and casually challenged him to see who could flip those coasters closest to the wall. Bobby took home about $50 by the time they were through. There was hardly a game he had not played some time in his life, even if not recently. As a boy his older brothers would trot him around making bets with strangers using Bobby as the prop. Yes, he had played the game of "coasters closest" in his youth.

What people didn't know was he was very good at getting the tension out as he would say. He told me once on the golf course, "Renée, golf is about getting the tension out. I have been working on getting the tension out for 50 years." Could he ever. On the putting green he would say, "Renée, when you look at a putt, you can't say, 'I think I can make this putt.' You have to say, 'I know I can make this putt.'" He had exquisite control over his body.

One time on the course at Fresh Meadow Golf Club in Long Island, playing with Alan King, the famous raconteur and comedian, and my good friend Steve Levy, Bobby announced, "I have cancer all over my body. They cut my balls off (he had metastatic prostate cancer), I am on this terrible chemo, I am so weak I have to play from the front tees." So we let him. And he proceeded to win every hole, striking his drives off the tee 200 yards in the middle of the fairway. He was winning all the money so we huddled and decided, "Bobby, we have to move you back, you are winning every hole." So we moved him back to the white tees twenty yards back and he commenced to hit his drives 220 yards right in the middle of the fairway.

We looked at each other, then at Bobby, and Alan said, "Bobby, what's going on? We moved you back and now you hit it to exactly the same place as before."

Bobby, in his high, squeaky voice, squealed, "Well, you moved me back, I had to do something."

Many tennis fans, and others, speculate about whether Bobby threw that match to Billie Jean in the Astrodome that fateful night in 1973. Bobby was capable of anything, but I can assure you he did not throw the match. It would have been stupid to do so. Besides the $100,000 winner-take-all prize, if he had won the victory would have been worth millions to him—in assorted endorsements, appearances and contracts. To lose meant infamy, the label of loser, to a woman no less—even if she was a champion and younger than he. And as crafty a hustler as he was, he was even more a proud tennis champion. He would never have lost in front of millions watching. In fact, I know he bet a sizable sum on himself to win. So why did he lose? Besides the fact Billie was younger and a great champion, and one of the best money players and greatest competitors in the history of tennis, men or women, he lost, in some part, because he took her too lightly. He had beaten Margaret

Court, at that time the number-one-ranked woman in the world, easily. He thought Billie would be even easier. But he underestimated her. Bobby had done a crafty psychological ploy on Margaret, enticing her into a match she thought was to be no more than an exhibition at a tiny club in the San Vincente Mountains east of San Diego. Then, at the time of the match, she realized what a bonanza media circus it was to be, and was ill prepared to do battle with Bobby. He beat her 6-2, 6-1, and presented her with roses. A real psychological beat down.

All his friends said, "Bobby, Billie Jean is no Margaret, she is going to be ready for you. Thousands in the Astrodome will not bother her, it will enable her. You better train, this is Billie Jean King." But he didn't listen, and all he did was go around promoting the match, no practicing. His friends implored him, "Bobby, this is Billie Jean King." He didn't listen. They went into the Astrodome in Houston, then the largest indoor stadium in the country, a tiny tennis court erected in the center of a vast arena, hardly any backdrop to visualize the ball coming at him, squinting with his eyes behind his thick glasse, Billie Jean serving and volleying like a champ. It was best of five sets, but it was over in three straight—6-4, 6-3, 6-3. He jumped over the net and kissed her. He had asked for a rematch. He never got one, why should he have?

There is, of course, another side to the argument about whether he threw the match or not. Some say Bobby did not care about preserving his reputation as a great player, that having won almost every match a man could win as amateur or pro his legacy was secure. They argue he was more interested in the bet, the scam, the chance to make money, lots of it. Some say he bet much more on himself to lose than he did to win. They argue, "Why would he agree to a best of five set match against Billie Jean?" He would certainly know he would have little chance against a young opponent in a five-set match. So he agreed, knowing it would not be a long match because he was going to throw it. When he lost in straight sets, he jumped over the net to congratulate Billie Jean— another jab at the world.

People who know tennis and more importantly, who knew Bobby, remember him fondly. He was an inveterate hustler at anything, but he was generous and at dinner he would often pick up the check. But the thrill of victory was what spurred him, and he had to bet, on anything and everything. He once told me (in golf), "Renée, you have to play for something. Even if it's only pennies, you have to play for something."

Often negotiating a bet would take longer than the match itself. Once, when I had only recently moved to Newport Beach, California, and was playing at my new club, the John Wayne Club where several top pros were members, Bobby came waddling out with his pigeon-toed gait onto my court exclaiming, "Renée, hey, it's great to see you. The guys said you had moved out here, but I didn't know where. I will pick you up in the morning and we'll go down to San Vincente and play some guys a practice match." Bobby had it all figured out, no one knew who I was; he could sucker some guys into a big bet. Sure enough Bobby was waiting outside my condo at Promontory Point on the coast highway in the morning and off we sped down the San Diego Freeway to the little club in the San Vincente Mountains (the same club by the way where he had beaten Margaret Court before the Billie Jean match). When we arrived, two guys were on the court waiting as Bobby announced, "I brought myself a partner, let's have a practice match, a thousand a corner." (That's $2000 for our team against theirs.) He introduced me as Renée Clark (sometimes I used that name before my real name, Renée Richards, became known after that LaJolla match disclosed my identity).

Our opponents looked me over suspiciously and one of them said, "Okay, let's see her hit a few balls first." They didn't recognize my name nor my face.

Bobby turned to me and said, "Renée, they want to see you hit a few. Do it, but not too good."

I complied, rallying back and forth gently a few minutes until one of our adversaries said, "Okay, let's play."

Bobby and I beat them easily in straight sets. As soon as the match was over, Bobby said to me, "Renée, get in the car, I will get the money." No drinks, no dinner, no congratulations, no conversation with our foes. Just, "Renée, get in the car." I complied and within seconds Bobby was behind the wheel speeding up the freeway to Newport Beach. Another hustle for Bobby Riggs.

Only once did I know of where Bobby got out-hustled himself. Len Hartman, who owned the Hi Way public tennis courts in Brooklyn, set up a money match between Bobby and Steve Ross. Bobby did not know who Steve was, but anyone familiar with local eastern tennis in the New York area in the '60s and '70s certainly did. He was the best player in the eastern section for several years; he had wins over many highly nationally ranked players, but he had never ventured onto the major circuit where he might have become well-known. Moreover, he looked like a homegrown public park player (which he was), not much style, weak serve, hit the ball with all kinds of spin with a weird grip. But he was a genius on a tennis court—swift, great reflexes, and shrewd like a billiards player. He used his opponent's power and redirected it back against him, like a t'ai chi master. He grew up in Miami, Florida, and didn't play tennis until he was 16, and then was self taught, and after a few years he moved to New York City. Players joked that his competitors in Miami paid to get him to move north. He then became unbeatable in the New York area. I can attest to his genius. I lost to him too, and I had been one of the best eastern players (men) for years, even winning the prestigious NY State Men's Championship in 1964.

Bobby was brought by Len Hartman to observe Steve play, and what he saw did not impress him so he agreed to spot Steve three games and play for $50. When Steve beat him, he asked for a rematch; he would give Steve a two-game spot. Steve beat him again. Then he asked for another rematch, with a one game spot. Steve beat him again. Whereupon Bobby said he was going home and would return the next day and they would play even, no spot. Steve beat him again. Then Steve gave Bobby a one-game spot, and beat him, then a two-game spot and beat him. Finally, there was a seventh set, and here history gets muddled. Most remember Steve won that one too—winning all seven sets, but there are those who say Bobby finally won the seventh set with the three game spot. Either way, he had been taken.

Steve, of course, was Bobby's junior by 25 years. However he was so deceiving because of his appearance, his style of play and lack of international career, that it was not surprising Bobby had misjudged him. Nonetheless, true to form, he turned the episode into his advantage, and introduced Steve to Hank Greenberg, the baseball star who loved tennis, Jack Dreyfuss, the multimillionaire investor, and many money doubles matches including Steve and Bobby resulted.

To illustrate how deceiving Steve Ross could be, I have to mention one memorable match involving him. One time, it was winter 1980, when I was coaching Martina Navratilova we needed a practice court on a specific hard surface for an upcoming tournament indoors. The only one I could find was in a large indoor club with several such courts far from Manhattan in the far end of Brooklyn, The Paedegaat Club it was called.

When we arrived for our practice session, I noted on the board in the lobby of the club the list of its directors and there was written, "Head tennis pro Steve Ross." I was delighted. I told Martina, "An old friend of mine from eastern tennis is the teaching pro here; maybe I can get him to play you a practice match." I always tried to find good men players to play her in practice before a tournament. She agreed and I sought to locate Steve, who was on the court with some kids in a coaching clinic. He was pleased to see me, and when I asked if he would play Martina he readily agreed. I told her, "Forget about the way he looks, this guy can play." Steve, a little paunchy, his tournament playing days behind him, belly sticking out over his baggy shorts, balding head, trim moustache, did not look like a tennis champion. They started to rally, and by the time they played the first point I looked around and it seemed like a hundred young junior tennis players, boys and girls, had gathered, surrounding the court, watching. The word was out—"Martina Navratilova is here and she is playing Steve."

They started to play and before Martina knew what was happening Steve was redirecting all her powerful shots back to her side, putting her on the run with her own power. His two-fisted backhand, which looked makeshift, was hitting winner after winner. In ten minutes he was leading 3-0.

Martina looked over at me and yelled, "I cannot play this guy. He doesn't hit the ball anything like anyone I have to play."

I said to her, "Martina, listen, forget what he looks like. It's a ball, a court, just play the point and forget the way it looks. It's a great experience for you." To her credit and to her sense of herself as a great champion, she rose to the challenge and the set became memorable—especially for all the kids observing. An aging local tennis genius toe-to-toe with the greatest women's champion of all time.

Finally, they got to 6-6 and Martina yelled, "Tie break."

Steve, out of breath, and out of leg strength, waddled up to the net and shook her hand, "Martina, thanks, I gotta go. I have a lesson to give. I can't play the tie break. I enjoyed it."

Martina turned, peering into the crowd, and yelled, "Where, where is the lesson?" She wanted to finish him off.

I said, "Martina, that's enough. Steve has had enough. You both did great." In The Paedegaat Club in the outlands, the hinderlands in Brooklyn, no less.

In 1976 I was in the middle of my efforts to be allowed to play on the Women's Pro tennis tour, and more important, to be given entry into the U.S. Open Championships at Forest Hills, NY. I was not having much success; the Women's Tennis Association and the United States Tennis Association were blocking my entries. I had stopped practicing ophthalmology while I was pursuing my battle for acceptance as a woman tennis player. And I was going into the poorhouse. No income, debts to pay, my financial future bleak.

Then, out of the blue, my manager, David Buffum, came to me and said, "You have been offered $250,000 for a match with Bobby Riggs at Caesar's Palace Hotel in Las Vegas. The match will be in two weeks. The limousine will pick you up and take you to the airport. Be ready."

I was living at my father's house in Forest Hills, where I had grown up, at the time, a five minute ride to LaGuardia Airport, then a few hours by air to Vegas. I said, "No." I thought David Buffum was going to kill me. Out of work, out of money, we—he and I—had no visible means of support. He was staying at my father's part of the time too. And I tell him, "No."

I had not lost my mind. It was a tempting offer, for sure, and money like that would take me years to earn. The offer was made because the promotors thought a match between Bobby Riggs, who had lost that famous match to Billie Jean, against the infamous woman, former man, Renée Richards, who was trying to play on the women's tour, would be a natural for public interest. But for me, and I think to this day I was right, it might have doomed any chance I had for a legitimate claim to play on the women's tour. If I agreed I thought it would mean the end to my chances in the NY State Supreme Court to be allowed to play in the U.S. Open. It was not easy to turn down all that money. And not even safe for me either. The "break a leg" guys in Las Vegas had a money interest in a match with Bobby. The bookies, the promotors, stood to make a lot of money. They didn't take lightly to someone refusing an offer, spoiling their chance for a payday. Nonetheless, I survived, home, in the house of my childhood, until a better day.

Fast-forward to the summer of 1977. Judge Alfred Ascione of the NY State Supreme Court decreed I was to be admitted into the U.S. Open Women's draw, and given permission to play on the WTA professional tour (which I did for four years, until I started coaching Martina.) I had refused to play Bobby for $250,000 in 1976, but very few people know that in 1978 I actually did play him. Two challenge matches, each for $2000 to the winner, in London, Ontario, in July, in a fairgrounds, where a temporary court had been erected, with makeshift metal stands for the few thousand fans who turned out to watch. Two matches, $2000 each, in a fairgrounds in Ontario. No TV, only local reporters. I was already an established player on the tour; my reputation would not be in jeopardy to play anyone anywhere. I agreed to the match. It was over the July 4th weekend, our matches just part of a big weekend (it being Canada notwithstanding), horse races, amusement rides and games, all part of the festivities. The first match was on Saturday evening, under the lights—if one could call them that—four poles situated at each corner of the court with a few klieg lights blaring from them. It was a very close match, which I won 7-5, 7-6. Bobby was giving away 15 years to me and, by this time, I was on tour and very fit.

We played the second match the next day, Sunday, at high noon, and the sun was burning on the black cement court. Bobby did not want to lose to me again, Ontario or not, and he remembered having beaten me once in a mens match years before. But I beat him again—this time 7-5, 7-5. We both came off the court totally exhausted. We went underneath the metal stands that had been erected on one side of the court. There was shade from the burning July sun and it was a little cooler there sitting on folding chairs on the cement floor. Bobby looked like he couldn't move, he just sat there, wiped out—and disappointed that for the second day in a row I had beaten him. I had never won Wimbledon, never been the number-one player in the world. He just assumed he could keep on being the best, no matter the age of his opponent. I knew how he felt.

I consoled him, "Bobby, I am on the tour, I am fit, I am younger than you, you did well to play me as close as you did."

And then he looks up and says, "Renée, you played great, I know, but now I have to go out and play the Canadian junior champ."

I was astonished. I said, "What are you talking about?"

Bobby had arranged to play a match against Mike Puc, the Canadian junior champ, after playing me. He was to get a good fee for doing that. He said, "Yeah, I said I would play him after you."

I looked down at him sitting on that folding chair, almost unable to get up off it, and I said, "You are nuts, you can't even move. I will play him for you myself."

Bobby looked at me and in his even squeakier than usual voice, mumbled, "Would you do that, Renée?"

I went out and found Mike Puc, a strapping eighteen-year-old Canadian kid, and said, "Look, Bobby is wiped out. He can't play you, but I will. You have to give me two games a set because I am pretty wiped out too from the match Bobby and I just played."

He says, "Okay, I will play you, but no spot, no handicap."

I said, "You have to be kidding. I am almost as old as Bobby and I have been playing in the heat for two hours already."

He says, "Sorry, no games."

So we arranged to play one set, no spot, if it were tied at 8-8, then a tie break. Which is what happened, and at 8-8 he beat me in the tie break. Was I mad. I could have killed him if I had started fresh. But at least I saved Bobby from getting heat stroke or a heart attack, whatever. That's what happened in London, Ontario, one July long ago. And hardly anyone knows about it except me.

I remember several memorable matches I saw Bobby play when he was young against the best players in the world, but they did not involve me. There was one, however, when he was in his fifties that did. I was playing at my club in Newport Beach one day when Bobby showed up with a friend and waddles over to me saying, "Renée, why don't you find yourself a partner and we'll play a practice match (practice = money, of course). I looked at whom he had brought along to be his partner. It was Frankie Parker, who had won the U.S. Nationals (before Open Tennis came in '68) at Forest Hills in 1945. It was during the war and he was Sgt. Frank Parker of the U.S. Army at the time. When he showed up at the John Wayne Club with Bobby that day, yes, he was well past his prime, but he could still play pretty good doubles.

I said, "Bobby, where am I going to find a partner to play you and Frank here?"

He replied, "Renée, find one of your friends from the club."

He had no idea, but I had a secret weapon. I called up my friend Betty Ann Stuart, wife of the club pro Ken Stuart. She was a very strong player, but not one of the Virginia Slims players known to Bobby like Billie Jean or Margaret Court. He didn't know how she could play. I said, "BA (that was her nickname), I have Bobby Riggs and Frank Parker over here at the club. They want to play a money match, can you come over?"

She said, "Sure, maybe in about ten minutes."

We had begun to play some doubles together after I joined the club, and we made a very strong team. Almost as tall as me, very strong, young, she could stand up to men players, especially fifty-five and older ex-champions. After introductions the four of us went out on the show court at the club, which was sunken below the surface of all the other courts, so viewers could watch from a high angle the action down below. It had an electronic scoreboard, and someone quickly put up on it: Richards-Stuart vs. Riggs-Parker. Club members stopped their games and gathered around the seats just above the court below.

Two out of three sets, tie-break at 6-6 in the third if needed. In those days the tie-break was best of nine points—first to 5, not the first to 7 as it is now. The first set went to Bobby and Frank. Both very steady, they made very few errors, lobbed over our heads when we came to net and played like the crafty veterans they were. We got going in the second set, and won it with strong serving and put away volleys at the net. We were women and they men, but being younger and stronger, we had the heavier artillery. The match went to a third set and we had some torrid exchanges, Bobby and Frank chasing down all our smashes and big forehands. The set was tied at 6-6 and we started a tie-break to decide the winner. We were behind 4-2. They needed only one point to win. I served an ace to Frank, 4-3. We won a long point to tie the tie-break 4-4. Frank served to BA and she cracked a screaming winner forehand return past Bobby at the net for the win. We had beaten Bobby Riggs and Frank Parker in a challenge match on the center court at the John Wayne Club. Bobby and Frank came slowly to the net. They didn't know what had hit them; they were dazed. Handshakes and kisses exchanged. The electronic scoreboard recorded the result (and stayed displayed for a few weeks after). Bobby paid the $200 for his team to me, and I gave BA her $100 share for the win. Bobby and Frank were stunned; no drinks, no shower, they just got in their car and left. How were they to have known that the makeup club team they played, hopefully for an easy afternoon's payday, would later that summer become the finalists in the U.S. Open Doubles Championships at Forest Hills, losing to Martina Navratilova and Bette Stove in a tie-breaker?

When BA and I stood on the podium at Forest Hills that beautiful Indian Summer day, September 1977, holding the bouquet of roses in one hand and the silver ball emblematic of being the finalists in the national championships in the other, the band playing, the fans in that old ivy-covered stadium, the last time the U.S. Open was ever held in Forest Hills, cheering, I turned to her and said, "BA, next year we will be back for the gold ball as the winners." And she said to me, "Renée, you will never get me back here again." True to her word, she went back home to Newport Beach, played at the club, taught juniors on her court at home, tended to her garden, and had another son who would become a tennis champ—Taylor Dent, who had a good career as one of the last serve and volleyers in men's pro tennis.

So many stories about Bobby and of so much the public has so little idea. He was a great tennis champion, but his legacy will always be clouded by that match in the Astrodome with Billie. His friends loved him, and when he was on his death bed, his body racked with cancer, they crowded around him crying. He looked at them and said, "Don't feel sorry for me. I played tennis and golf my whole life. Don't cry for me. I played tennis and golf my whole life."

That's the One I Can't Stand

Coaching Martina Navratilova, arguably the greatest woman tennis player of all time, was always a "trip," a challenge. Highs, lows and in-betweens, the time from my retirement from playing, in 1981 to start coaching her, to my return to the practice of ophthalmology in the middle, to getting fired from coaching her in 1983, and rehired in 1987. I could write a book about it all, but I won't. A few highlights stand out and at this time of my life—my memory and concentration not being the greatest—I will recount just a few.

The first real highlight was when Martina won the French Open in 1982. Not considered a great clay court player because she was a serve and volleyer—which meant steady ground strokers with good passing shots had the advantage on the slow clay courts, neither she nor I were sure she could prepare to assault the red clay courts at Roland Garros in Paris and win. In fact, one of the reasons I started coaching her was because I watched in disbelief when Chrissie Evert beat her 6-0, 6-0 on the clay in Florida at Amelia Island and I thought to myself, "This cannot be." Martina could play on clay. Didn't they have all those clay courts near Prague where she grew up? She just didn't know how to play on clay. So we worked on that and in the spring of 1982 I got her ready for the premier clay court event in the U.S.—the Family Circle Cup in Hilton Head, South Carolina, the lead-up event to going across the pond for the French Open. And part of the working included exhausting physical conditioning—clay court matches can last for hours—the points take so long, with players able to run down and return almost all of the balls bouncing on the clay. We would practice the corner drill, where I would stand in one corner and Martina would have to return my shots—to anywhere on her side of the net—to my corner. I would run her from side to side, front and back, and she had to hit every shot back to my corner.

At first she could do it for only about ten minutes and then she would hang over the side of the low fence gasping for breath. Gradually fifteen, then twenty, and finally a half hour—first with me standing in one corner and then the other. When she could finally do both corners— a half hour each—I said, "Okay, you are ready for the Family Circle Cup." Harbour Town at Hilton Head in the spring is beautiful, flowers in bloom, visitors from cold climates filling the town, the beach, and the week of the tournament a festive time. Martina, still unsure of her ability on the clay, especially after that blanking double "bagel" at the hands of the best clay court player in history—Chrissie Evert—only the year before, started tentatively. But soon she realized that first of all she knew how to play on the clay, and secondly she had the stamina to do it. I told her, "Martina, if you win the Family Circle Cup you can win the French Open."

Well, she won one match, then another, and another, and all of a sudden it was Saturday night and she was in the final of this country's premier clay court event on Sunday afternoon, with Bud Collins, famed tennis writer and commentator, getting ready for his prime time TV in the tower at the end of the court, built to broadcast the event. I came back to the condo where we were housed during the week after dinner, and at ten o'clock I walked in to see, to my astonishment, fifteen or more women athletes, basketball players, golfers, all friends of Martina's and her friend, basketball star Nancy Lieberman, partying to beat the band. I froze a moment, and then, in a voice about two octaves lower and two decibels higher than I had used in years I announced, "Ladies, Martina is playing the final of the Family Circle Cup at noon tomorrow. This party is over." They turned and looked at me, jaws dropped, and one by one they filed out. Martina went to bed, got up refreshed the next morning and went out and won the final. I congratulated her and said, "Good, let's go to France."

The French Open may be the most difficult of the four major tournaments that comprise the grand slam of tennis. On clay, the matches last longer, the friction of the ball on the clay retards the speed of the ball after it bounces, allowing a player to catch up to the ball and hit it again, and some times points last more than a minute, some rallies can consist of twenty of more shots before a point is won. For spectators the advice is, "Bring sandwiches." Steadiness, consistency, stamina, all give the advantage to the steady baseline player, one who rallies from the baseline, steadily without error, and who does not often play by venturing to the net to volley—where the opponent can hit a passing shot or a lob over one's head. Matches are often wars of attrition, exhausting battles

142

of hours of rallying back and forth, no one putting the ball out of reach for a winner. European and South American players brought up on clay who have learned a steady baseline game have the advantage. Curiously, however, in the twentieth century the best woman in the world on clay came from Florida (Chris Evert), and the best man from Sweden (Bjorn Borg). Winning the French Open at Roland Garros would be a feat for Martina mostly because her style of play favored serving and rushing the net to volley, good for grass courts like Wimbledon, not so good for the slow red brick clay courts at Roland Garros. Roland Garros?—a World War I French flying ace—the French Open referred to colloquially simply as Roland Garros.

When we arrived in Paris I attended a magnificent dinner in one of those gigantic restaurants on the Bois de Boulogne—the big park in the middle of the city. I ran into Jean Borotra, one of the famous four horsemen, the four musketeers of French tennis fame in the 1920s. He was 90-plus then, but I had met him once before in the1950s when he played in our National Indoors Championships in the 7th regiment armory in New York City.

I asked him at the dinner, "Jean, do you think a woman can win the French Open serving and volleying?"

He thought a moment and then said, "Renéeee," in his inimitable French drawl, and then again, "Renéeee, eet ease a beeg court, Renéeeee, eet ease a beeg court." Translation: Renée, it is a big court—meaning that for an average woman's size, there is too much court on either side of a player rushing the net for her to catch up to passing shots on either side of her. She would be passed most of the time and lose the point. I thanked him for his advice.

At the same dinner I ran into my old friend, the Australian champ Lew Hoad—whom I had met years ago at his tennis ranch in Mihas, Fueringola, in Spain. One of the most sensational players ever to play the game of tennis, his longevity cut short by back problems, he will never be known as the greatest of all time, but ask any of the old Aussies who was the best player of their experience and most of them say Hoadie without missing a beat. And that includes the great Rod Laver, who won not one but two grand slams, the only player in history to do that.

When I ran into Lew Hoad at the dinner I asked him, in a slightly different way, "Lew, did you serve and volley when you won the French Open in 1956?"

He replied without missing a beat, "Renée, you cannot do what you don't not know how to do." Translation: Of course I served and volleyed, that's what I do. I thought about it, a lot, and about how I used to play on clay, and how Martina had just won the Family Circle Cup on clay. And so it came to me. You play your game, sometimes you serve and volley, sometimes you stay back, depends on the opponent, depends on the score. You play your game. And if you are fit, you win. Which is exactly what Martina did.

Chrissie got upset by Andrea Jaeger in the semis, and Martina beat Andrea in the final. She had won the French Open—Roland Garros on clay for the first time. A magnificent victory over a sensational young star, Andrea Jaeger, whose future brilliance was too soon to be cut short by shoulder injuries, but there was a little drama still to unfold after the match. The press conference at major championships brings reporters from all over the world, crowded into the interview hall to question the players. I always refrained from attending them after Martina played. I thought she should be up there reveling on her victory, or explaining a defeat—on her own. And this time, as usual, I went and sat in the players' lounge.

About fifteen minutes later, Nancy Lieberman, ex-pro basketball player and Martina's friend at the time, came running into the lounge yelling, "Renée, Renée, you have to go in there. Andrea said she couldn't beat the three of us, and Martina is crying."

Evidently Andrea was upset that Nancy and I were cheering for Martina from the "friends" box in the stands, and she felt like we were coaching her—giving us an unfair advantage over Andrea, who only had her ex-boxer father, Roland Jaeger, cheering for her. So I broke my rules and walked into the room, facing literally 200 reporters from everywhere. In French, I said Martina had won Wimbledon before I ever began to coach her, she won this match on her own, Nancy and me cheering for her had nothing to do with the victory. Speaking in French to the French assembled was a good idea. The situation had been defused.

Team Navratilova—as Martina's entourage was beginning to be called—Martina, friend Nancy, coach Renée, friend Svatka (from Chicago via Prague, who cooked delicious Czech dishes for Martina), Aja Zanova, the ex-Czech Olympic figure skating champion, agent Peter Johnson, nutritionist Robert Haas, friend movie director Milos Forman (*Amadeus* among other great movies), and a few other friends I can't even remember settled in two houses Martina rented within walking distance to the All England Tennis and Croquet Club for the Wimbledon fortnight. And Martina won again, this time for the second time, of nine overall—the record for men and women to date.

After the finals the press crowded around me, and the question was shouted, "Dr. Richards, Dr. Richards, what are you going to do now that you have coached a Wimbledon champion?" expecting me to say I was going to open an academy for junior tennis players, or continue on tour with Martina, or in some way capitalize on the victory.

I answered, "I am going back to New York to resume the practice of medicine (opthalmology)."

And of course I did just that. A colleague in my subspecialty (pediatric ophthalmology and strabismus) had just died, his widow in charge of selling his practice and office had been told by her friend, well-known ophthalmologist Virginia Lubkin, the best bet to be able to take over her husband's practice was Renée Richards—however, she was not available because she was in London coaching Martina Navratilova at Wimbledon.

The widow was miffed, but she said, "Call her anyway, we will wait." So she had friends call me and with a modest—for then—price of $50,000, agreed upon, put forth by Martina, by the way. As soon as the fortnight was over, I flew back to New York to start practicing medicine on my own again.

The 1983 French Open was hardly as much fun as the great victory of 1982. Firmly entrenched in my new practice at 40 Park Avenue in New York City, and operating at both the Manhattan Eye and Ear and the NY Eye and Ear hospitals, I had little time to travel with Martina, so I only came to isolated events, and then even not for the full length of a tournament. In the spring of 1983, Martina defending her great 1982 victory at Roland Garros, I could only attend for what I thought would be the important second week, and I flew to Paris on the middle Saturday for her fourth round match against Kathleen Horvath, expecting to stay for the second week hopefully for quarterfinal, semifinal and final rounds. It never happened. Kathleen Horvath was an excellent player, but Martina had never lost to her and as I raced from Charles de Gaulle Airport to Roland Garros and settled into my seat next to Nancy Lieberman, who had assumed some of the role as helper if not actual coach to Martina, I was ready for an exciting second week of the French Open, Andrea was there, and of course the great Chris Evert, too.

The match with Kathleen was a disaster from start to finish. Kathleen was not missing a shot, and she ran down every one of Martina's balls on the slow red clay. They split the first two sets and started the deciding third. Suddenly Nancy got up from her seat and moved a few rows down in the stands, starting to encourage Martina on her own. Martina looked up, from Nancy to me and back, not knowing where to seek encouragement. She lost the third set and the match; the defending champion out in the fourth round. A disaster. After the match she was inconsolable; she cried, Nancy cried, and I was beside myself. All I remember is scribbling a note to Martina something to the effect I couldn't compete with Nancy as her coach. In essence I fired myself, before Martina could do it for me. The ecstacy of victory and the agony of defeat—1982-1983. I was fired on the spot. I didn't even check into the hotel. I never unpacked. I simply went back to Charles deGaulle and took the next Air France jet back to NYC, back to my office, back to the hospitals.

It was not until 1987 that I was to return to coach Martina for the summer majors. We had kept up with each other. She was coached 1983 through 1986 by Mike Estep, and then briefly by Peter

Marmuranu from Rumania. In fact, during the U.S. Open one of those years—'85, '86?—I was in Southampton, Long Island, at the beach for Labor Day weekend when I got a call from Martina, frantic, that she was playing in the U.S. Open and she couldn't see the ball—her glasses were no good. The call was on Sunday afternoon of the three-day weekend. So I drove back to New York City, met Martina at my office Sunday night, examined her eyes for glasses, called my good friend optician Art Leonard—who made up a pair of glasses to the new prescription, and had them ready for her for her match on Monday, Labor Day. Martina was very appreciative I cut short my Labor Day holiday to come back to the city on Sunday to examine her in the office. I told her, "Listen, you bought the office. You can use it when you wish."

In 1987 she asked me to come across the pond, as they say, to coach her for the French Open and for Wimbledon. I agreed to take two weeks off from work to do it, but returned to New York in between the two tournaments in June. The French Open was once again a disaster, but not like 1983 when she lost that match to Kathleen Horvath. This time it was the final round, and her opponent Steffi Graf. It was a great match, and Martina was within a point of winning it. She took her eye off the ball with an easy volley, very close to the net, Steffi far, far away near the end of the court, and put the ball into the net. Martina never recovered and ended up losing the match with a double fault. I always felt the pressure of having so many of her entourage to pay for at the $1000-a-night St. Cloud Hotel contributed to the burden she felt on the court. There was Martina, her friend Judy, Judy's parents Sarge and Fran, Judy's brother little Sarge, Judy's two kids, and a few others I don't remember. Whatever, Steffi was a great player so no excuses needed in losing a thriller to her. Still, a heavy toll for me, in the airport in Frankfort on my way back to New York for a few weeks between the French and Wimbledon. All I remember was the newspaper kiosks and the Frankfurt papers blaring four letters across the entire page—G-R-A-F. I can still see it.

Wimbledon 1987 was not going to be another heartbreaker. Martina owned Wimbledon, the grass courts, the little club across the road from Wimbledon where many of the top players practiced, the town, she was the queen of the All England Championships, nine titles there in singles overall. When I returned from New York I settled in to one of the two houses Martina rented a short walk from the All England Lawn Tennis Club. In the first house was Martina, Judy, me, Svatka (who cooked up some great Czech dishes), and Martina's mother and father. In the second house were Aja Zanova, Milos Forman, Peter Johnson (Martina's agent), boxing champion Sugar Ray Leonard and his assistant, Joe Breedlove, Martina's sister Jana and her husband, and maybe a few more I forgot.

Martina played great throughout the fortnight and as it came down to the final few matches I felt good about her chances, Steffi Graf looming on the other side of the draw notwithstanding. I did take the precaution however to impose on Neale Fraser—the great Australian lefty who won Wimbledon a few times—to come over to the practice club to give Martina a few pointers on lefty serving, which he did willingly and fruitfully. The day before the final I asked Emilio Sanchez, the great Spanish champion who hit a forehand hard like Steffi, to play a few practice sets with Martina. His coach Pato was always so helpful.

Whenever I would say, "Pato, I need Emilio for a practice session with Martina," he would say, "Okay, Renée, Emilio, Javier, same thing." And of course he would have either Emilio or his brother Javier, who hit the same forehand, available for me. Emilio showed up this time, but so did Jana and her husband, Aja Zanova, Paula Smith (a top player and friend of Martina), Sugar Ray and Joe Breedlove, all with their own racquets, dressed for tennis—asking, "Renée, where's my practice match?"

I looked at them, astonished, and said to all assembled, "Whoa, slow down, slow down, Martina is playing for the Wimbledon Championships tomorrow. Today is for her to get ready with a few practice sets with Emilio. I promise you, after the match tomorrow, I will have games arranged for all of you. And so they trooped off to the sidelines to watch the practice, and then the next day to see Martina avenge her loss to Steffi at Roland Garros, with another championship at Wimbledon. Sugar Ray told me how excited he was to be part of it. He said tennis was much like boxing, how he could see in the eyes of his opponents when he had them beat. I am sure he saw in Martina's eyes that Sunday that she was going to win.

I flew home to New York for the second time, happier on the flight from London than on the one from Paris. Martina had won Wimbledon with me coaching her—1982 and now 1987. She had won the French Open with me coaching in 1982, but 1983 and 1987 had been tragic defeats. I returned to my office, by then I was very busy with my practice, surgery, teaching, seeing patients in the office, knowing I would coach her only one more time—later that summer at the U.S. Open in Flushing Meadow in Queens, New York City. I could drive there from my apartment each day of the tournament, no transatlantic flights necessary.

The Sunday before the tournament started I had booked a practice court in the stadium (at that time it was the old Louis Armstrong Stadium, Arthur Ashe Stadium not yet built). Seeded players had the privilege of booking an hour of practice in the stadium; they were most likely to be scheduled there during the tournament. Our court was for 6 p.m., still plenty of daylight left. As we dressed for a practice in the players' locker room I hurried to put laces in a new pair of sneakers only a few minutes before our scheduled time.

Hana Mandlikova, who had won the U.S. Open in 1985, was there, she saw me struggling with my shoes, and promptly took one of them and began lacing it up for me. She said, "You have a practice time in five minutes in the stadium, you will be late."

With her help we made it to the stadium on time and as we walked through the runway to the court Martina looked up and stopped a moment, exclaiming, "It's not the same, it's just a mass of steel and cement, and it's not so special." She was comparing the stadium court in New York to the one at Wimbledon—ivy-covered walls, thatched roof, gorgeous grass court, steeped in tradition.

I thought to myself, "This is going to be difficult; Martina is not enthused, she is not excited to be here, she has won this event before, and it's not Wimbledon. She is not motivated. We are in trouble."

We walked out onto the court, put down our gear by the netpost, and started rallying with each other from the baseline. I wanted to warm her up and then play some points with her, serving and volleying, like she would have to do to beat Steffi Graf again, should they both reach the final. Nothing happened. It was like a movie in slo-mo. Martina was simply going through the motions of practice, no energy, no enthusiasm, no passion, no drive, just rallying back and forth without interest. We were indeed in trouble. After about ten minutes of meaningless rallying all of a sudden I heard a voice behind me. Unforgettable if you have heard it before. John McEnroe called to me from the runway; he had booked the court after us.

"Hey, Renée, let me see if I can win a few points from Martina." John McEnroe—who grew up in Queens like I did, who had watched me play local tournaments when he was in the boys and then juniors, who had become one of the greatest players of all time, and certainly the greatest player ever from New York—was fast coming onto the court behind me.

I turned around, facing John, and said, "John, hi. Sure, come on out and play some with Martina."

So out he came and he and Martina began to play points, first one serving and volleying for 21 points, and then switching and the other serving and volleying for 21 points. It was like a light switch had been turned on in Martina. From a listless, disinterested participant in a practice session of no interest, she suddenly became rocket star Martina, running, hitting, attacking every ball. There were a few workmen scattered around the stadium, and a few other players and their coaches standing around too. They all stopped to gaze on what was happening on center court, the night before the U.S. Open.

The greatest man server and volleyer of all time squaring off with the the greatest woman server and volleyer of all time, both left-handed, in front of a handful of people standing by, entranced by what they were witnessing. It was a happening, just by chance. Martina was keeping right up with John, serving that slithering slicing serve out wide, and coming in to the net to make one beautiful volley after another. John, not holding back, hitting his great lefty serve, wide to the deuce court and wide out in the add court, coming in to put away one volley after another. It went on for a half-hour, absolute concentration on both sides, everyone observing knowing they were witnessing something special. I stood near the umpire stand, my mouth open but in silence, along with the rest. Sudddenly after John had served about twenty great serves, followed by twenty great putaway volleys; he hit a volley into the net. In a flash he took his racquet and threw it the length of the court, smashing it into smithereens on the wall at the end of the court.

I was standing not far away from him near the net and I looked at him stupefied. I blurted, "John, you just hit 20 perfect first volleys for winners into the open court. You just missed this one."

Whereupon that look came over his face, that look of anguish, like when he would look at a linesman who made a bad call and he would shout, with his hands on his hips, agony on his face,"You cannot be serious." and he turned to me and said, "That's the one I can't stand." Not good enough to hit 20 perfect volleys for winners, he wanted to hit them all for winners.

Martina watched. She absorbed. She learned. She became enthused and motivated. The tournament started on Monday and she kept on being enthused. She reached the final against Steffi Graf at the end of the two weeks and served and volleyed her way to beat her in straight sets to become U.S. Open champion again.

And I thank my friend John McEnroe for showing her the way.

Best in Show

My coach, Frank Froehling, sent me up to Gainesville, "To learn t'ai chi." I didn't know how long it would take—for some people in China it is a lifetime. Frank thought maybe a weekend. It was about a two-hour drive northwest from where we lived in the old plantation on the brackish St. Lucie River, near where the NY Mets baseball team takes spring practice at Port St. Lucie. Gainesville, home of the Gators and the University of Florida, is in the middle of the northwest part of the state, Alachua County, prairie country, halfway from the gulf, halfway from the ocean, redneck country it is said, except for the university in town. When I arrived I was sent by the t'ai chi master to be quartered as a house guest of another t'ai chi student, one Melissa Vinson, who was, I am certain, the only adult in Gainesville at that time who had no idea who Renée Richards was. Cousin of Carl Vinson, the longest running member of congress in history, and distant cousin of Chief Justice of the U.S. Supreme Court Fred Vinson, she was not much of the world at large, certainly not the pop world.

After three weeks I returned to Frank's home, where I had been living with him and his girlfriend Deborah, to pick up my stuff. He didn't even ask, "Where have you been for three weeks?" He just asked when I would be going back up to Gainesville. I said tomorrow, and after I packed up my belongings in my little compact Buick, I headed back north. I didn't know it then, but I was to stay in Gainesville two years. Melissa and I found a house to rent—$250 a month when we could afford it. We studied t'ai chi, practiced yoga, chanted, I trained in tennis, and we were part of a small group of young adults joined together loosely in Arica— we were seeking enlightment and not just from t'ai chi. Arica may be compared to EST or other such mind-body-spirit cliques—but very small, and a lot more sophisticated than most, if I do say so myself.

Even if Melissa had no idea who I was, the word spread quickly. This was 1979, I was almost a household word, and I was invited to play an exhibition against a man who was the tennis pro at a small private club—The Devil's Court, close by the sinkhole of the same name—The Devil's Millhopper. Ed Leach and I played in front of the members of the club, and several young people from the university

152

community one Sunday afternoon. I remember I won the match. Ed would soon take over the job of coaching me, Frank back in St. Lucie, and Ed continued Frank's torrid physical training schedule for me, as well as playing me practice sets several times a week. I remember only winning a handful out of maybe fifty sets we played during that time. That I had won that first exhibition match was not surprising at all. I had that effect on people—I was the "bad gun in town". I can only imagine how Ed felt when he played me that first exhibition.

Ed became my coach, he even traveled to a few tournaments with me, but it was his brother Jerry who became my closest friend— besides Melissa of course—while I lived in Gainesville. Jerry, slightly older than Ed, not as educated—no college for him—nor as sophisticated, he was what a stranger might call a redneck, but then if that had really been true why would he be best friends with Renée Richards?

Jerry was a good tennis player, not in Ed's class, but he was good practice for me and we would play often at the Gainesville Golf and Country Club, where Jerry was the pro. A strange scene—the one waspy, snooty club in all of Gainesville and who is out on the court playing—Jerry Leach and Renée Richards. The women of the club were cordial to me, but not exactly embracing. I think Jerry was asked not to bring me around after the first season we played there. I didn't care that the bluehaired ladies didn't warm to me. The one member who was always warm and friendly to me was the biggest celebrity in town. That was Roger Maris—who broke Babe Ruth's single season home run record in 1961.

I would watch him practice his golf swing sometimes and when he would loft a booming drive I would yell, "Way to go, Roger, another Ballantine blast"—the way radio announcer Mel Allen used to shout it—just like the home runs I had seen him deposit into the right field bullpen in Yankee Stadium some years before.

He would smile and say, "Naw, just a pop-up, Renée, just a pop-up." He was retired; he had owned the Budweiser beer distributory in Gainesville after his baseball days were over.

Jerry and I were not the only slightly out-of-place characters to grace the country club, and not including the occasional rattlesnake that would slither through the fence onto the burning hot cement tennis court and get unceremoniously decapitated by Jerry's tennis racquet. Also present frequently was Mike DeFranco, Jerry's protégé, age 17 and a tennis genius. Mike lived with Jerry and his wife Pat, in town, his own father lived in the Virgin Islands. I don't remember a mother having much to do with him, but a grandmother lived in Florida not far away. Mike was an up-and-coming junior amateur until he was declared a pro for accepting some prize money at a tournament and that ended his college scholarship aspirations.

When I came to know him in Gainesville I helped him to renounce his pro status, become again an amateur, and helped him get a scholarship at the University of Central Florida. That didn't last long, mostly for reasons of personality, which will soon be evident. Back in Gainesville he just lived with Jerry and played tennis. He was a true tennis prodigy. When I came along I befriended him, practiced with him, and coached him some. Talk about odd couples—people would stop and watch—first at the Country Club, then at The Devil's Court Club where I was a member, and anywhere Mike and I could be seen hitting with each other—We were quite a sight—here was this 6-foot-1-inch woman with heavy booming ground strokes, trading shots with this short, skinny, hardly more than 150 pounds, scrawny kid. His face always scrunched up, contorted, marked by acne scars, and in contrast to me with my rather orthodox, yes, classic strokes, he had a rather unique style of hitting a tennis ball. Two-handed backhand not so unusual, but his forehand was hit with a bent arm throughout the swing, almost all the power coming from his body rotation. And he stood inside the baseline to hit almost everything, right after the bounce, it required exquisite timing. Even returning a 130-mph serve, he would stand right inside the baseline. He was quick as a cat, and his eyes were uncanny.

When I would go off to a tournament and see some of the men on the tour I would often compare them in my mind to Mike, he could play as well as the best. It never happened, of course, and no one has ever heard from him, but not because he couldn't play. And he could play all day too. He didn't lift weights or stretch or run, but he jumped rope for an hour at a time. His diet a was little unorthodox, too. A dozen donuts for breakfast washed down with five cups of coffee. I tried to coach him; actually I was the only one in town he would take any advice from. He knew I knew tennis. He wasn't dumb. In fact, ask him anything about the Civil War or the two world wars and he could recite battles chapter and verse. I didn't coach his strokes, his were unorthodox but they worked for him, and I couldn't change his diet or his habits either. I just tried to help with tactics, strategy, playing matches. It was very frustrating.

I would arrange practice matches for him with friends of mine, good players, kind enough to come over to Devil's Court and play Mike. Often, after they had split the first two sets, Mike would get in his little Fiat convertible, drive home, snort up, and come back for the third set. Invariably in the middle of the third set he would pick a fight with his opponent and that would be the end of the match.

I would tell him, "Mike, you can't do that; these guys do me a favor to play with you. I am running out of opponents for you."

He couldn't help it. Mike Oransky, great guy, had been a very good college player; he was the pro at the municipal courts in town. He told me, "If that guy keeps getting nuts I am going to flatten him."

Next time they played Mike DeFranco didn't like a baseline call on the far side. He couldn't have seen it from where he was anyway, and he came around the net and went after Mike Oransky. It was all I could do to separate them. Once I entered him in a tournament in Jacksonville, about an hour east of Gainesville, where he lost to another young player, then picked a fight with the kid's father in the parking lot. I got him out of Jacksonville fast.

Mike moved in with Jerry and Pat and they became essentially his guardians. He was only 17. They took care of him like a son. Jerry's reward for all his kindness to Mike? Mike picked a fight with Jerry right in the living room of their modest house. Not too smart on Mike's part, but he just couldn't help himself. Jerry had been lightweight boxing champion in the U.S. Marines. Not much bigger than Mike, he knew how to fight. He knocked Mike out cold, one shot to the chin. Jerry used to tell me he loved fighting in the Marines.

He said he loved "getting hit in my tiny little Irish nose. It felt good." Hard to imagine. Mike moved out soon after that, and it was not long after that I left Gainesville myself. I missed him. I always dreamed of him making it on the tour someday, me coaching him. And he had been very loyal to me; he respected me, he would go after anyone in a bar or a club who who would make insulting remarks about me.

Jerry worked for another year after that as the pro at the Gainesville Golf and Tennis Club and then he took a course to become an inhalation therapist. He had had some experience as a helper to the Navy corpsmen at the field hospitals when he was in the Marines during Vietnam. Jerry is the only guy I ever knew who signed up for a second tour of duty in 'Nam—he had so much fun the first time. He got himself a good job in a hospital in Gainesville and he and Pat moved to Archer, just outside Gainseville, a redneck town one might say. Pat had worked for a veterinarian; she had helped me with my Airedale, Tennis-ee, who was a handful, when he was just a pup. I remember she always said, "Airedales are easily distractible"—how sage that was. She always had a Diet Pepsi in hand, and the three of us hung around together—until finally it was time for me to leave my life in Gainesville—The Devil's Court, Arica, the duck pond, the prairie, the Gators, and once again return to a different world—Park Avenue, NYC, the Manhattan Eye and Ear, the world I had left five years before to commence my journey into the world of tennis, and the public eye. I left Jerry and Pat, and a few other close friends—some I would never again see.

It was four years later when I got a call from Jerry, from Archer, Alachua County, Northwest Florida: "Hi, Renée, it's Jerry. Pat and me, we're coming to New York to the dog show with Pete."

I said, "Pete?"

He replied, "Yeah, Pete, he's our Australian Cattle Dog, we're gonna bring him up to Westminster."

I took a deep breath. "Jerry, what do you mean? You are going to show your dog at the Westminster Kennel club dog show?"

"Yup, we arrive on Sunday; cattle dogs are shown Monday afternoon."

I knew from Westminster, at Madison Square Garden, the most illustrious dog show in the USA, maybe the world unless you like Krufts in London better. A dog has to be a champion to even be eligible for Westminster. And usually there are handlers, groomers, kennels full of more than one dog—it is a big business. One can't just show up with a solitary dog from home, back there in Archer, Alachua County, I would have added had I had my tongue at the moment.

I said, "Jerry, great to hear from you. Do you know what you are doing?"

He laughed, and said, "Pete is the best Australian Cattle Dog in the country. He won his championship down around here in the South. Now it's time for the big one. He will win. We will have a ticket for you at the box office; it will be great to see you."

Jerry had never seen me as a civilized, even well-respected doctor before. He only knew my address, 40 Park Avenue. It was all he needed to know about his friend—he would say it over and over, 40 Park Avenue, like it was a title. He loved that address. I could only imagine Jerry and Pat—and of course Pete, at the Westminster Kennel Club Show, the kennels with stables of dogs, the judges wearing evening clothes evaluating the dogs running around the ring kept in tow by professional handlers.

I knew from Westminster, I'd gone several times to watch the Airedales in the show. And once when Butch Seewagen showed his Newfoundlands. I told Arleen about Jerry and Pat. Arleen was still friendly with two of the breeders of our Airedale, Lily. She mentioned to them what I had related about Jerry and Pat. They laughed, that derisive laugh that says, "Are you kidding me, some redneck ex-tennis pro brings up his lone cattle dog to show at Westminster?" Like "haroomph."

I walked from my office on 36th and Park to Madison Square Garden on Seventh Avenue and 33rd Street, the entrance teeming with humanity, and got on the long line to the box office. Within minutes I spied my old friends Jerry and Pat coming toward me. "Renée, it's us, come on." We embraced, so happy to see each other. Four years hadn't changed us much, only the clothes and Jerry was wearing a tie. They gave me my ticket, we entered the hallowed halls of Madison Square Garden—I knew it well, the championship fights, the Knicks basketball games, the concerts, the rallies, the rodeo, the circus, I had even played there in World Team Tennis, and coached Martina there in the year-end Women's Pro championships. The Garden—the tops, and especially in the dog world.

I met Pete in the kennel section one flight below the show ring—actually rings plural—there were three for the best in breed competition. Only on the second night when best in show is contested does it become one big ring. Now to my eye, no expert on Australian Cattle Dogs, Pete looked, I would say, okay. Australian Cattle Dogs are not exactly English Setters or French Poodles, or…Airedales even. Just an ordinary-looking dog—not handsome or pretty, certainly not cute—but I do admit he looked like the kind of dog you wouldn't want to cross or so it seemed. Moreover, he didn't look distinguished or special. I glanced at the other Australian Cattle Dogs, all gray, short rough coat, curved tail, average size 50 pounds, short ears, moderately pointed snout, not long. They were real dogs, truly, dogs not to be trifled with. But not breathtaking.

The time came—"Will the Australian Cattle Dogs please come into the ring?" And there was Jerry—owner/handler as it had said in the program, with his tie on, Pete in tow, jogging into the ring, along with 15 other Australian Cattle Dogs. Some breeds have fifty or more in the show, like the Labrador Retrievers, but some have a small field, even the Airedales had only about 20. Of course, every dog in the show a champion. Jerry jogged around a few times with Pete, in the middle of the group of cattle dogs. I will admit I couldn't tell much difference between any of them, except Pete did seem a little more purposeful, like he knew what he was doing, on a mission. I mean he gave the impression he didn't come all the way up from Archer for nothing.

And then, just like that I see the judge pointing to Pete, motioning him to the front, and then another two dogs behind him. "One, two, three," said the judge, pointing at his choices. The judge placed a blue ribbon on Pete, Best Australian Cattle Dog, Westminster Kennel Club-1984. I swear, by that that time I was not even surprised.

I had stood by when the Dutchess of Kent handed Martina that magnificent plate on center court, Wimbledon, 1982, the first time I coached her over there. I had been pretty excited. But no more than I was watching Jerry Leach stand there with Pete—at Madison Square Garden—at the Westminster Kennel Club—Best in breed, Australian Cattle Dog-1984.

Jerry and Pat took me to El Parador, one of New York's most famous Mexican restaurants, close by my office, on 34th and Second. What a celebration. I don't remember too much of what we said there or much about the burritos and the tacos because I passed out on the floor for a few seconds from too many margaritas. (How does anyone know how much tequila is in those things anyway?)

But I do remember when I woke up, I did say to Jerry, "Well, next year you will be back with Pete to win the best in show—not just cattle dogs, but Airedales, Newfoundlands, Boxers—all the breeds."

Jerry laughed and then he said, "No, Renée, it was great to see you, and we are happy for Pete. But we had enough New York. Once is enough .We will never be back." And that was the last I ever saw of my dear and loyal friend from Gainesville. I had a call from his brother Ed only a few years later, and he put Jerry on the phone to say hello. He didn't know the brain tumor he had would take his life a few weeks later.

And Mike DeFranco? That same year I got a call from a tennis pro at a club in Western Massachussets. Mike had been teaching juniors up there for a few years. He dropped dead from a drug overdose, and the only known living person the tennis pro knew to call was me. I wrote out a eulogy and they read it at Mike's funeral.

He could have been best in show too.

Closet Queen

I met Robert in Fred Shaw's parlor in the apartment he rented in an old brownstone house in Brooklyn Heights, NY, just across the river from Manhattan. Fred was host to a motley collection of mostly misfits—men—some in various stages of transgenderism, others with only a cross dressing story to discuss or hide. They would meet monthly for a discussion session—exchanging experiences and stories about their other lives as would be women. From various walks of life, some poor, some rich, some educated, some sophisticated, some not. A motley collection.

Some were just thinking about embarking on the arduous path toward a sex change operation, others were partway there—having taken hormones for a few years already. A few of those came dressed as women, all the others as men. Only a few were young, one about twenty, I remember; some were middle-aged. A few were just observers, not in any kind of hormonal treatment, not even contributing stories of their own, just looking on and listening. There would be dropouts, never to be heard from again. Some returned on occasion, others were regulars. Some reported on the progress of others they knew. The worst tale I remember was when one middle-aged man reported on Ray McCaffery, who had been a high school science teacher, married, two kids. Ray had had the "operation"; he became depressed. He said "he wasn't any more a man or a woman." Two months after surgery he killed himself. I never forgot that. It was just when I was beginning to think a sex change was right for me, and I had met Ray at a few of the sessions.

This was in the beginning of the 1960s, hard to believe now with Internet access to hundreds of agencies and information sites, but actually back then the only focus group—support group—for the transgendered in all of New York City was Fred Shaw's informal periodic coffee klatch (for wont of a better phrase to describe it). He had been printing a soft cover magazine a few times a year called "Turnabout"—in his basement printing press beneath his apartment on the first floor there in Brooklyn Heights—mostly stories written by men (no women) who wanted to be women or pretended to be, who had found Fred via the underground grapevine in Manhattan.

Dr. Harry Benjamin, the father of transsexualism, Christine Jorgensen's doctor (and mine), the only doctor in the country known for taking care of transgendered people (although neither that word, nor even transsexualism, which was coined by Harry, had yet been invented) suggested I might want to attend a few of the sessions of the group. He knew my need for privacy; indeed, all his patients needed privacy back then. But maybe he figured I needed more because I was a physician, and he thought Fred's sessions would provide that and also give me some acquaintance with others in the same boat as me. I went to some of Fred's meetings for about six months, on and off, listened more than spoke.

It was at one of those sessions that I got to know Robert. Tall, dark hair, dark eyes, rugged, quiet, he was what we called then an observer—he just looked like an ordinary person, but who knew? Maybe a transvestite or someone dreaming about a sex change. The unusual coincidence that we were both physicians probably sparked our friendship, but in those days, even in the safety of Fred's parlor, everyone was so secretive about any private wishes or thoughts that could be considered deviant, there was rarely any frank discussion of what anyonelse's problems were. Neither Robert nor I ever appeared at a meeting dressed any differently than as in our public lives. Two young physicians, athletic, I would say goodlooking, if I do say so myself.

I didn't know his last name then, but that wasn't unusual given the circumstances of our acquaintanceship. I eventually learned he was a resident in orthopedic surgery and had played college basketball for an Ivy League team. And he did confide he had a girlfriend one evening after a meeting at Shaw's when he opened up a little about her over a few drinks at Pete's Tavern in Gramercy Park. He said he had met her only the year before at a mixer at Sarah Lawrence College (a mixer is where young people from all over the city come together to meet over Cokes and potato chips, mostly to meet potential dates), just north of the city in Bronxville in Westchester County. Neither he nor she had anything to do with Sarah Lawrence, he from the Ivy League and she from a city college in Manhattan. At the mixer she was surrounded by eager young doctors, lawyers, advertising men, stockbrokers and editors, but he managed to have said hello, and obviously made an impression, because when he called her the next day she was willing to meet him for a date. He was one lucky guy. She was beautiful—long sandy hair, perfect features, almond-shaped hazel eyes, great figure. They fell in love quickly and became inseparable. He called her Jeanie Peanut Butter for no reason I ever knew. She was still at college when they met and living at home in the city with her parents. Her father I learned, and this is really crazy as will become apparent later in this tale, was a renowned psychoanalyst in New York City, a refugee from the Holocaust. He even had known Sigmund Freud. He was not a slave to Freud, however. He called himself eclectic—Freudian when it was appropriate, Jungian sometimes, sometimes just common sense psychotherapist. She lived at home officially, but soon after they met she spent most nights at Robert's apartment uptown in the 80s on the East Side.

And every night invariably she would say, "I have to call my mother," to lie to her and to say she was staying overnight with her girlfriend. Her mother knew better. She liked the young orthopedist and knew her daughter was in love.

Robert told me more about Jeanie Peanut Butter than about himself. When she dislocated her shoulder fencing in college she was admitted to Lenox Hill Hospital, only a few blocks away, for surgery.

She wouldn't let anyone draw blood from her arm for the pre-op blood test. She simply said, with resolution, "Get Robert up here, I will only let him draw the blood from my arm." And so Robert was called, and he did it. And then he relocated her shoulder under anesthesia and put it in a sling. No operation.

He told me she was a beautiful pianist, having graduated from the High School of Music and Art before college, and she no longer played, except for him. On rare occasion he would sit enraptured by her playing—Chopin, Mozart, even the Tchaikovsky Piano Concerto. They were inseparable, and so in tune with each other they hardly had to remind each other of dates or meetings, each one automatically knew when and where to show up. But she never cooked for him.

Damndest thing, but she told him, "After we get married I will cook for you every night." What's that called? I forget. Something about holding a promise or a threat or something like that. Emotional blackmail? No, gastronomic blackmail maybe.

After college he shifted from basketball to recreational golf, even played a few local amateur golf tournaments, and she was always by his side. The other players loved her, why not? Beautiful, playful, and Jeanie Peanut Butter and Robert were expected as a pair.

It was while they were still living in his apartment she found out. Called a studio apartment, only one long room it was, with a Pullman kitchen (like in the cars of the Pullman trains of the last century—a wall kitchen at one end of the room). The bed was at the other end, near the window looking out on the side street below. It had only one closet. One day, he was at the hospital late, still a resident surgeon in training, and she chanced to open it and to her utter surprise there were a few dresses hanging on the rack, pushed off to one side. She was astonished, I can only imagine. In disbelief, shock, fright, she did not know what to think. Were they the clothes of another woman? That could not be, Jeanie was the only one ever there. But, yes, she did go home to her parents' apartment sometimes, that was a fact. Could they be Robert's? Robert with dresses? Unimaginable. She sat down in shock and waited.

He came home, late, there had been emergency surgery, he was exhausted. To be confronted by his sweetheart finding dresses, not hers, in the closet. Oh my god. What could he say, how could he explain it was true, they were his? But that is exactly what he said. He had been dressing in women's clothes compulsively since he was a teenager, sometimes only rarely. He always tried to control the urge, and only a few times in his life did he ever venture outside dressed as a woman. He had no idea why he did it, it was not to attract men since he was an ordinary heterosexual male, he just couldn't help himself. He was embarrassed beyond imagination to have to tell her, but he did. She didn't really have much to say, he recalled, when he told me about her unmasking of his secret.

She just thought a moment and volunteered, "Yes, a dress can be a very secure feeling." (Sure, for a woman, not a man!) They went to bed, made love, and fell asleep.

He did have this compulsion, he said, to dress up as a woman, but that was about it. And he kept it under his best possible control, all through college, medical school, athletic competitions, and secret from anyone and everyone—family, friends, girlfriends; it was his cross to bear. Once, in medical school he sought out a psychiatrist, so distraught he had this uncomfortable, only partially controllable, energy-sapping compulsion.

The shrink had no idea what it was all about. He asked, "Why don't you wear a flower in your suit jacket lapel instead?"

Robert gave up on seeking help. He just lived with it the best he could. He would try to get help in the future, maybe.

Only once did he lose his grip on the urge. He was sharing a summer house with a friend in East Hampton. This guy, Neil, was always looking for action, he was always calling girls for dates, with limited success. He would eat breakfast in the coffee shop on the first floor of the Barbizon Hotel for Women, where all the young model hopefuls would stay in New York City. He liked to have Robert go there with him and, if lucky, to double date with him.

But this one time Neil wangled a date for himself, but not for Robert. Left alone in the summer rental in East Hampton—it was no palace, not on the ocean (they were struggling young residents at the time), it could be a little dreary—and without a party taking place. He became depressed and lonely, and resorted to his stash of women's clothes and dressed up. And he couldn't control it. He went outside; the one no-no, the one absolute prohibition. If you have to do it, do it alone. Not being an expert at makeup, wigs, dress or shoes, it is not hard to imagine the sight of him marching along the main street of Amagansett, Long Island, in drag.

When some teenaged boys walked past, one of them took a look at Robert, pointed, and yelled, "Queer."

That was it, Robert went berserk, attacked him, punched him in the face, and they fell to the sidewalk, arms flailing. I can hardly imagine the scene—Robert pummeling his hapless tormenter, his dress not concealing the rage within. East Hampton policemen arrived. Robert was unceremoniously and shamefully handcuffed and put in the back seat of the police cruiser—wig askew, dress torn, lipstick all over his face, which was buried in his hands.

Neil was called to the lockup in Riverhead, the county seat, where Robert had been taken and put behind bars, in his torn dress, with two cellmates, both half passed out, but they were dressed in shorts and T-shirts, appropriate for their sex—male. Neil stupefied, Robert mortified. But Neil not so stupefied it would keep him from bursting out laughing, which I am told is exactly what he did. More important, however, is he then accomplished the feat of not having the episode blasted all over the *Hampton News*, the local newspaper, testament to his cunning, quick thinking, and almost certainly also the result of a conference call to Larry Levine, one of NY's top lawyers, who knew Robert, had even seen him about his bad back a few times. Robert was let out, in the custody of Neil, lucky for him—no beating, no sexual assault. Good thing it was Riverhead on Long Island and not Rikers Island in New York City, where The Tombs would not have been a fun experience, to put it mildly. No misdemeanor charge, no morals charge, no assault and battery charge. In those days any of these might mean a loss of one's license to practice medicine in NY State. Remarkable. Still don't know how he got off.

Robert was never pugnacious; the eruption at having been called queer had just set him off. In fact, he was just the opposite, a peacemaker. One time in Chuck's Composite, the bar and restaurant frequented by models and other young New York sophisticates, Neil and Robert were at the bar when two guys got into a fight over a girl they were trying to impress.

Robert just got between them, one strong grip on the arm of one and one on the arm of the other, and suggested they calm down. "Come on, you guys, this is a restaurant, take it easy, lots to enjoy here, calm down." Which they did.

Robert and Jeanie never talked about his secret in the closet, never any psychological discussions, questions, nothing, never.

The only reference ever made was on rare occasion when she had to go home at night to stay at her mother's home and she would say, "You aren't going to do stuff while I am gone now, are you?" And he would promise, "No stuff."

And she did know he was seeing a psychiatrist, an eminent Freudian psychoanalyst, a few times a week. It was not unusual at the time. It was not uncommon for educated bourgoisie young adults with anxieties, phobias, compulsions, to seek to ameliorate them, undo them, via psychoanalysis, especially in New York City. She left the issue up to his analyst, although she didn't really care, it had nothing to do with their life together the way it was. She had mentioned it to her father in confidence when she first found out and she had taken his advice. The old man was pretty savvy. He had observed his daughter and Robert closely, had been on vacations with them, and knew they were in love. He told her to carry on her life as usual, and this from an analyst as eminent as Robert's.

Their romance continued through his residency and her last years at college, all their friends as well as family assuming they would soon be engaged and married. The other residents teased Robert about being so slow to propose. They were all married, and she was ready too. Quite ready because when she missed a period it seemed like the time had come—marriage and a family soon would be forthcoming. But not for the psychoanalyst—the attending shrink, not the father in law…unfortunately.

By the third year of psychoanalysis Robert was well under the influence of Dr. Braun. Not exactly robotic, or mesmerized, but he was a willing participant in the analytic process, and took to heart the interpretations that accompanied the wafts of cigar smoke from behind the couch up there in those spatial quarters above Park Avenue, where the doctor had not only his office but his elegant apartment adjoining. Armed with the imprimatur of being the president of the most important psychonalytic society in the country, reputation as an expert on fetischism, Viennese accent,

167

picture of Freud in the waiting room with piercing eyes trained on the patient sitting there, from any angle, same cigar in his mouth it seemed as in Dr. Braun's. How could his dictates, supposed to be only interpretations and observations, not be taken to heart?

No, he did not look like Freud—he was large, seemingly immense, with a bald head, sometimes wearing his glasses and no beard. But he did have that accent, and the cigar was the same. No piercing eyes like in the picture, because the analyst always is seated behind the patient on the couch, but Robert never forgot that—from anywhere in the waiting room there was Freud staring at him. You know, like the Mona Lisa without the smile.

Robert would sit in the waiting room, always harried from having to race from the hospital to make the appointment on time—6 p.m. in the midst of rush hour on the streets below—God forbid he was late—"the lateness is motivated" he was reminded—subconscious resistance to the therapy it was called. And he was always alone in the waiting room, God forbid another hapless patient could be seen, or see him, waiting for his or her session. When the door to the smoke-filled analyst's room would open, Dr. Braun would say nothing, simply stand aside and Robert would dutifully take his place on the couch, his eminence seated behind it, and free association would start. Free association meant Robert started talking, and kept right on until on rare occasion the doctor would comment or offer an interpretation. Sometimes the entire 50-minute hour would consist of Robert talking (or just lying there and not talking), and nothing coming forth from behind the couch except the cigar smoke. What a process, for three years, and the poor son of a bitch would always come back for more. If it wasn't mesmerizing I don't know what to call it.

When the session was over Robert would get up and leave the office by a different door than the one he came in by, no one to know he had been there. Only it didn't work perfectly because once he caught a glimpse of another patient just having arrived in the hallway outside the office, mistiming the careful schedule to ensure that never happened. It was someone he knew, had gone to high school with him, even on the basketball team. He was a young psychiatrist; this was his training analysis, with the great man. Shhh.

When she missed her period, Robert reported it to Dr.Braun and then spent almost the whole of the next session talking, with no repy from behind. He said he was happy, they were in love, and now they would get married and start a family.

Finally the doctor spoke, rather pronounced, "No, you can't." One time when he actually spoke. He went on, "Not with your problem, not with your compulsion. These things are sticky." (Exact words as related by Robert.) "We have to explore it." In other words, he was telling Robert there must be no marriage, not yet, and the pregnancy had to be aborted. He said Robert would be doomed if the baby was born and they got married, doomed if, "They" didn't get to the root of his compulsion—his dressing up on rare occasion at home when his sweetheart was absent—"doomed." What the doctor was really afraid would be doomed all right was the analysis, the sessions, the material for him to write another paper about the young professional man with the well-compartmentalized psychosis who was already making him even more eminent as the subject for papers in the psychoanalytic quarterly. Have the baby and everyone is doomed.

The sessions became heated, less down time, less free associating, more talking, arguing, it had deteriorated, degenerated. It became hardly a Freudian analysis; it had become directional therapy. Anti-anxiety medication was advised (also rather unorthodox for a Freudian analysis). There were dictates, threats, and screaming—from both couch and chair. This went on for two weeks, Freudian analysis was supposed to be non directional. This was breaking a cardinal rule—no dictates. Of course Freud was quoted to have said to his followers, analysts who trained with him, "You are Freudians, you cannot be directional. But I am Freud" (meaning he could do whatever he wanted). And that was Dr. Braun evidently too. Anything he wanted. It was also an axiom that no life-changing decisions could be made during the time of analysis—like having a child. Of course having an abortion might fit that description too.Moreover, another point about Freud. He didn't trust young people in love. Dr. Braun went along with that for sure.

In the end there had been enough brain washing, enough influence, enough coercion, enough weakness, enough exertion of power—the doctor behind the couch won out. Just like that. The young doctor on the couch caved. Like not with a bang but a whimper.

Jeanie was distraught; no more than Robert, but it was she who was carrying the baby. Abortion was illegal, and even if it weren't she didn't want one, and she knew Robert didn't either. How could he be so weak to cave in to that horrible man? Even her own father knew they were meant for each other; of course he had no idea what was growing in her body at that time. And he was only the father-in-law to be—not Robert's doctor. The doctor on the case had decreed, "Get an abortion. The analysis must continue." His fame would grow, he would write up the details, expound his opinion on the case to analysts worldwide. And the poor son of a bitch, brainwashed on the couch, bathed in cigar smoke, never had a chance. He would arrange the abortion.

Robert told Jeanie the dictate—get an abortion or else. Or else what? He did not know. He was following orders. She became enraged—she bolted from the apartment and ran toward her parents' apartment on the West Side, Robert in pursuit. She didn't go into the building, she ran down to the park adjacent to the river and he ran after her. When he caught up with her he held her in his arms. She was sobbing uncontrollably. He just held her, nothing could be said. What could possibly be said?

With the Supreme Court having not yet heard Roe vs. Wade, abortions in this country had to be arranged outside the law. Sometimes a nurse practitioner, sometimes a doctor—in a seedy section of Queens, or far out in the middle of New Jersey. Most enlightened (?) young New Yorkers knew someplace where it could be done. None of them appealing and all of them risky, in less-than-safe or unhygienic conditions. An abortion was outside the world of their ordinary sphere of life. Robert researched the possibilities, one such in Queens seemed the least dangerous, but still—the doctor was not a certified gynecologist and the "procedure" (a D+C—dilatation and curettage of the uterus) would be done in his office, after hours, not in a hospital. Robert went there; he checked it out and became more depressed. He couldn't go ahead with the arrangements.

He asked around, again and again, and finally learned there was a place in Puerto Rico where it could be done, in relative safety, by a gynecologist, in a hospital. He called, he made the arrangements. He bought the tickets for Jeanie and for himself. When they arrived in San Juan—he had been there a few times on vacation trips—he knew where to tell the taxi cab driver at the airport. "Santurce, please, Calle Villaverde," and gave him the address of the doctor's office. Santurce, the town adjacent to San Juan, was not as big, not as cosmopolitan, more commercial, not a vacation place. The doctor greeted them in his office, asked a few questions about how "late" Jeanie was, why she wanted an abortion, what kind of doctor Robert was. He was miffed—a candidate for an abortion had never showed up in his office with the man who caused the unwanted pregnancy. And a physician to boot.

He asked them, "Why don't you keep the baby and get married?"

The answer simply, "We can't."

Arrangements made for surgery in the morning, admission to his private clinic in the evening, not exactly a hospital, but not a back room of an office either. "Nothing to eat or drink after midnight," he said, and then he got up and showed them out of the office. He was going to do it, but he did not really understand. He looked at the 400 USA dollars in his hand as he walked back to his desk.

They had dinner, mostly in silence. Robert and Jeanie embraced, she was admitted to the clinic and he sought a room at a hotel close by. He would pick her up the next afternoon, after it was over. Finding a slightly crummy hotel, he checked in and lay down on the bed. There was no way he was going to get any sleep.

"What are we doing? How can I let this happen? We love each other, we always have. There is no reason not to have a baby. Doctor's order? Who the hell is he anyway? What is going to happen if we have the baby?" He got up and went outside on the street, and found a bar close by, the door wide open, the neon light

171

above the door—"Abrea." He stood at the bar, drank a vodka, and then a few more. He found his way back to the motel and fell asleep with his clothes on, sprawled out on the bed.

When he awoke he looked at his watch and it read five o'clock. "Oh my god," he thought, "I have slept through the operation." He got up and ran to the door. He looked out. It was dark outside, and he started running down the street toward the doctor's clinic. And then he realized—there were no cars, there was no one on the street, the shops were closed. It was five o'clock, yes, but five o'clock in the morning. He kept running and running toward the clinic. He ran through the door, a watchman appeared, and then a nurse.

He was crazed, he was almost wild, he screamed, "Jeanie, Jeanie, Jeanie." And started looking in rooms. She appeared from behind a closed door. They embraced, and said nothing. Nothing had to be said. They didn't even exchange glances, just stood there in each other's arms. And then she ran back into the room, got dressed, and they were out the door in about a minute.

They walked to his motel, collected his suitcase, by then daylight was breaking and some people were seen about the streets. He found a taxi and said, "El San Juan Hotel," San Juan. They checked in and stayed for three days—on the beach, at the pool, in the dining room, and in bed. And then they flew home to New York.

They were married in a small ceremony, her parents and brother, his father and two best friends in attendance. The rabbi blessed them, their first child, a daughter, was born later that year. And then another, a boy, and then two more. He practiced orthopedics and taught at the medical school and played golf. She finished graduate school and raised her chidren. What had been in the closet in that first apartment was never mentioned, ever. Nor was the name of the famous pyschoanalyst who almost had had his way. Oh, and by the way, she did cook for him, every night—and kept kosher. They lived a happy life, Robert dying some years before she did. What would have been if he had not made it to that clinic in Santurce in time, who knows? And something else I wondered about too—what might have happened if Jeanie had died before Robert? You know, the closet and all that. Who knows?

The Last Trip for the 'Vette

Feb. 25, 2012

I knew it had to happen some day, everything changes, nothing changes, so it is said. I have had my 1967 Corvette convertible for 20 years and have loved it—driving it, caring for it, repairing it, babying it—only local driving, good weather only, and it was part of my persona, whatever that means.

Arleen advised, "Why don't you sell the Corvette? You have had it enough." She was right; there is a time for all things. "A time for all seasons." Too old to handle the no-power-steering wheel (teak wood though it may have been); too old to be comfortable with the stick shift, too nervous to take it on the interstate with semis—big eighteen-wheelers barreling down on you and blasting you onto the highway shoulder. Not to mention the fear of driving to Woodstock or some other pleasant day trip, only to have the engine stall and look frantically for a repairman. And the most important reason of all, my companion for 12 years beside me in the 'Vette, my faithful Airedale Travis, it was his car as much as mine, was no longer here—he died the previous summer.

It's a laborious process to sell a classic car—that is, if you advertise it, even online on UsedCorvettesOnline.com and then have strangers call, come and kick the tires, drive it around the reservoir, come back and say, "I'll call you." I never wanted to do that. By chance, I was talking to my friend Wayne Rider, who owns the local bank up here, on an unrelated matter, and he inquired about the Corvette. He is a car collector, and has several classics in a special house he built on the main corner of town. I told him I was thinking of selling it, the time had come.

He replied, "Take it down to Atlantic City, the big auction is this weekend. I bought two cars there the last time I went. Bought one, went and had a drink to celebrate, came back in and bought a second one."

It was a little late for Atlantic City this year—the auction was for the weekend, I had spoken to Wayne on Tuesday. But I figured I would give it a try. I called the office number of the show—Justin, the chief of the show, said, "Sure, Renée, bring it down, we'll sell it for you. No problem." No problem? Always a warning; anyway I thought, "Give it a try."

I called my friend Kenny the cookie man—Kenny Piersa—my buddy and golf partner, who knows cars, he owns a Pepperidge Farm cookie route in NYC. I wouldn't try to do this alone, but if Kenny could help I would try. He said he would accompany me. I called Passport Transport and arranged for transport for Thursday, the car to be auctioned on Friday evening. I got us hotel reservations at the Tropicana Hotel in Atlantic City for Friday night. I made sure my office schedule for Friday morning ended at noon.

Passport Transport arrived at 7 a.m. Thursday, and I drove the car up onto the platform, then Fred, the driver, used a remote to bring it into the van. He and his partner loaded the hard top, which Arleen and I had brought down from the shed, on the shelf above the car, and off they went to Atlantic City.

Kenny and I left Westchester County just after noon, stopped for lunch on the New Jersey Turnpike, a double Whopper at Burger King for each of us, and Kenny bought lunch for two Navy men on active duty who were in line with us—that's the kind of guy he is. We arrived in Atlantic City at about 3:30, checked into the Tropicana—what a zoo, you could get lost in there in a moment—corridors, towers, slot machines, escalators, restaurants, casinos, more slot machines, shops, but we found our rooms, left our overnighters, and headed for the Atlantic City Convention Center.

Gigantic. With no passes, no tags, no instructions—of course we were not preregistered—we were in a maze. But we found bidder registration. We were directed to the very back of the convention center floor, and walked, passing hundreds of magnificent collector cars on the floor to the auction office, and found the number where my car was—1535. We located the car—several prospective buyers surrounding it—and then the catastrophies began. First, it had not been detailed. All the other cars looked like they were still in the showroom, shined to a mirror glass finish—and mine with Putnam County dirt on the wire wheels. I went berserk, almost. We walked back to the office, and managed after some research to actually locate Justin, as I had pictured him, about thirty, long sandy hair, in his satin black jacket, running around, attending to details from hundreds of sellers like me.

"Justin, Justin, the car has not been detailed."

"Don't worry, Renée. I will have it done right now, don't worry."

And this was less than an hour before it was to go on the auction block. So we go back to the car and a guy says to me, "You know, something is hanging down underneath the chassis. It won't look good if you take it up on the block and the bidders at eye level see that thing hanging down."

So Kenny got under the car, yanked on the thing hanging down—a box about four inches in diameter, he broke it free from the wires to which it was attached. It was the old Maserati air horn I had installed years ago—it would blare "Le Marseillaise" alternating with "Dixie" when I would see a friend on the road in Carmel or at the golf club.

But that was the least of the problems. The real catastrophe was coming next. Someone asked me if I would pop the hood—he wanted to see the engine, and to verify the engine was the 350 hp, a very desirable option, and also to see that all the numbers matched. A collector car with all numbers matching—original engine, rear end, transmission—is worth much more than one with replacements.

I said sure and when I went to pull the handle to release the hood I found it on the floor with about 12 inches of the cable to the hood release extending from it. A true disaster, I could not open the hood. And even worse, the battery is under the hood, and on the battery is a turn off/on knob. Turned off, no way to start the car. Someone had evidently come by earlier, tried to pop the hood, not gently, and snapped the cable, leaving the handle and one end of the cable on the floor, not saying anything, to go off and probably destroy another car.

I was beside myself. I didn't even know whether the battery switch was on or off. On a chance, I put the key in the ignition, turned it—and the engine started right up. The battery had been in the on position. Amazing.

Two guys from Pennsylvania—car guys—became our friends; they tried to get under the car to release the hood. They found a roving mechanic who said he would have to jack up the car to get under it to work on the hood release. The jack he found was not high enough. The jack with the car was rusted and frozen. Kenny bought Heinekens for our two friends from Pennslvania. There were bar carts located all around the floor. They kept trying, but there was no way to get that hood open.

A guy came by and said he was a friend of Terry Feehan, a good friend of Kenny and me from Carmel. He said, "Call me when you get home if it doesn't sell. I will give you $30,000 for it." I told him I was putting a reserve of $40,000 on it for the auction, no sale if it didn't reach the reserve.

Then I had to make the first of the two crucial decisions of the evening auction—either postpone the auction until Saturday or Sunday in the hopes of getting the hood release fixed before it went up on the auction block, or drive it through as is, hood down. I calculated the chances of getting the hood release fixed before Saturday or Sunday—slim to none. To get a new cable from Long Island Corvette Supply Co. on the weekend, get it delivered to the car show in Atlantic City, and have someone install it within 24 hours—not likely.

My head was swimming. I am an ophthalmologist, a tennis player, golfer, I don't know from car auctions. Suddenly I just said to Kenny, "I'm driving it through." I got in the car, started up, and got on the line to the auction block, in my appointed number in line. People swarmed around the car. Several asked me politely to pop the hood for them. I told them I couldn't, someone had snapped the cable while looking at the car. I swore to them it was a numbers matching car. One guy said it looked like the hood was bent. "When was the accident?" I swore it never had an accident, not in my twenty years of owning it. One guy said he would give me $42,000. I should call him after the auction, So why not bid on it? I thought.

I inched it forward, suddenly Kenny hops in the passenger side. "I'm going up there with you." We got up onto the block. The auctioneer screaming into his microphone on Kenny's side, the assistant to the auctioneer on my side telling me what the bids are. It started at $30,000, and stalled at $32,000, went up to $35,000 and stalled again. The assistant asked, "Would I take 35." I said, "No." It suddenly went up to 38, and I was asked again—"Will you take 38?" I said, "No, I want $40,000." It went up to 39 and again I said, "No." At $39,500 the bids stopped. The auctioneer was about to say, "No sale," because it had not reached the reserve. The assistant asked, "Will you take $39,500?" And then I had to make the second crucial decision of the weekend. I said, "I"ll take it."

We drove off the block. Our buddies, the car guys from Scranton, Pa., said, "Congratulations, you did great." Could have fooled me. I was in a daze.

We found Justin. "Justin, it didn't meet the reserve."

He said, "Okay, I will cut the commission in half." We had to wait two hours for the papers to be changed to reflect the reduced commission—now only $1100. At 9 p.m. the woman who cut the checks gave me my check for $38,315. She said she was from Mahopac, next town to Carmel, go figure.

By then the cavernous arena with all those cars was almost empty of people. We walked by my car and I kissed it goodbye—on the hood. We realized the plates were still on it—my own personal plates, 819 R, my birthday and initial. We found a screwdriver and Kenny took off the plates for me to keep. We took one last look at the car. On the dashboard was a sign: "Rare find, 1967 Corvette convertible, 327 cc, 300 hp (wrong, it has the more rare 350 hp engine) power steering, power brakes (wrong ,it has no power assists) $49,000." Imagine the new owner trying to flip it, untruthfully, no sooner had it been sold. Lots of luck. Car auctions.

We had dinner at Dock's, a hundred-year-old Atlantic City landmark chowder house nearby, on the way back to the hotel, a superb meal of oysters, clams, crab meat, washed down with plenty of vodka (and gin for Kenny).

We figured we deserved to celebrate. I certainly could not have done it without him. And in the car on the way home I heard from our friend Terry Feehan—"Renée, congratulations, I heard you did great. You have a new career in sales. My friend from Mahopac said he saw you before the show and offered to buy the car for $30,000. You should call him back home. Then at 6:30 he calls back and says, "She don't need my help. She sold it for $39,500, never thought it would go that high." (Closed hood notwithstanding.)

It was quite an adventure. I thought all the Renée Richards stories had been told, guess not. New career? I don't think so.

The Last Day For Dr. Renée—December 18th, 2013

I got up at 5 a.m. It was still not daylight. I drove Arleen [and Rocco] to the train station in Brewster (usually twenty minutes), with black ice on the twisting roads around the reservoir, temperature still in single digits. This time it took a half hour. Drank my coffee and ate a donut on the way. Quick goodbye. Took the elevator up one level, (too old now to climb the stairs), bought my ticket in the machine, crossed over to the other side, took the elevator down to the track, and caught the 6:40 train to Grand Central. I read the New York Times on my Kindle, imagine that.

Used Arleen's metro card to get past the turnstile into the subway—only had to swipe it twice, not fast enough the first time—the commuter behind me in line impatient with my fumbling, squeezed into the No.4 train downtown, got out at Union Square, 14th Street and walked four long blocks, freezing, to the NY Eye and Ear Infirmatory (really Infirmary, but that's what I call it). Changed into my scrubs, and went to find my surgery partner Lisa. Lisa Hall, sweet Lisa, she looks like she is 16, petite, beautiful, soft spoken. Hardly. Looks can be deceiving. She is 50, the mother of two teenage daughters, a former registered nurse before she went back to study medicine, and arrived at the old Manhattan Eye and Ear hospital as one of my residents in training. She became a talented eye surgeon and now the director of pediatric ophthalmology at the Infirmary. We have been helping each other in the OR for fifteen years.

We went to look at our first patient in the holding area—really her first patient, me the assistant today; I did my own cases last week—a 17-year-old with a longstanding head tilt from vertical eye muscle imbalance. Only one muscle, an inferior oblique recession, a vertical, but easy, not a re-op, no scarring from previous surgery. Second case, a 52-year-old man with restricted elevation in one eye, sees double all over from vertical misalignment, had radiation years ago for orbital tumor on the optic nerve, now has radiation necrosis involving the inferior rectus. Put the inferior rectus on adjustable suture so we could wake him up, check position, and loosen or tighten the suture to change alignment of the eyes until double vision eliminated. Had quick bite to eat, tilapia, fried, very

179

good food at the Infirmatory, cafeteria open to one and all. Lisa paid for lunch—ten bucks for both of us. Third case, reop, 45-year-old woman, excited to meet me in holding area, tried to shake hands. I said no shaking hands before surgery. Three muscles, one the most complicated for surgery of all the eye muscles, the superior oblique. In the recovery room, patient, still groggy and uncomfortable, asked if I would sign her copy of *No Way Renée*. In recovery she asks me this. I said, "Sure". I wrote, "To -----, straight eyes are a privilege, and a right. Good for you. Enjoy, Renée Richards.'" Lisa does a beautiful operation on three muscles on one eye and the patient is asking me to sign her book. Then we brought the orbital tumor case back to the OR, adjusted him on the table, let the muscle slide back, too much, tightened it up, back and forth until he was fusing comfortably (using both eyes together without double vision), then we tied the suture and closed up. Fourth case, re-op, 35-year-old came in with his parents in the holding area. One muscle, but a re-op.

During the whole day Lisa is telling everyone she sees, "This is Dr. Richards' last day." I keep trying to shush her. Other surgeons keep coming up to me, between cases, during our cases, to say hello, goodbye, whatever, schmooze, congratulate, commiserate. Paul Finger, another former resident of mine, now one of the world's authorities on tumors of the eye and orbit, came in to the OR; we reminisced, even about the research operations we did on the monkeys at the now defunct Primate Center hidden in the woods in Rockland County. And after surgery, in the doctors' lounge, Brian Campolatoro, who is now the most productive eye muscle surgeon in the hospital, maybe in the country, kept saying, "Congratulations, Renée, congratulations." Over and over.

I was getting self-conscious. Even the staff, the nurses, the orderlies, she tells everyone. Rowena, my gentle and favorite scrub nurse, originally from the Philippines where most of our hospital nurses came from—we hugged and I felt like crying, only I didn't. At just before four I left the OR the last time. I looked around, the anesthesia machine, the electronic monitors, the video camera mounted on an arm from the ceiling (how often did I crack my head on that after surgery?), the operating microscope, the other machines around the room not even invented when I first learned to operate. And then I did not look back. I went up to my locker and changed into my street clothes, put on my boots for the slush outside, and walked the four blocks to the subway, squeezed and pushed my way into the rush hour crush into the No.4 train, one express stop to Grand Central.

I caught the 4:18 to Southeast—Brewster North on the Harlem line, the line next to that awful crash on the Hudson line. Arleen met me at 5:45 with little Romeo and Rocco. Long ride home, in the dark, Christmas traffic in Carmel the worst, roads not made for it. Home finally, shower, vodka on the rocks, dinner of roasted chicken and rice, and salad. Then a stupid movie with Robert DeNiro, called *The "Family"* about a mafia family relocated by the FBI to a countryside town in Normandy. Really stupid, but maybe not—the family can't seem to change its ways even removed from its familiar environment. But I wasn't even thinking about that, or about me, or about more than half a century in the operating room, thousands and thousands of kids and adults, maybe double the number of eyes, hundreds of residents and post graduate fellows learning along the way. I wasn't even thinking it's over. I just went to bed.

The End

About the Author

Dr. Renée Richards' life as the first athlete to play successfully in professional sports as a transsexual, to coach Martina Navratilova to titles in all four grand slam tennis championships, then to return to the practice of medicine as an eye surgeon (her original career) has been well documented. But her life included adventures less well connected to her notoriety, in her life as Richard Raskind, and later as Renée, in sports, medicine, her personal life, and in her connection to numerous personalities in the world. This collection of stories, starting with the gripping tale of a German spy suddenly appearing at summer camp, as well as anecdotes about baseball star Ted Williams, boxer Sugar Ray Leonard, tennis champion Bobby Riggs, and other well known people, include tales of dramatic medical emergencies, harrowing personal adventures, and some humorous anecdotes from a remarkable life.

The title story 'Spy Night and After' starts with Richard (before he became Renée) being sent to sleep away summer camp—and suddenly becomes a terrifying episode in the life of an eleven year old boy growing up during 'the War' when a stranger suddenly appears.

The author of this collection of stories is renowned eye surgeon and highly ranked tennis player, **RENÉE RICHARDS.** Born in 1934 as RICHARD RASKIND, Renée was thrust into the international spotlight for her sex reassignment surgery after she won a women's tennis tournament. Opposition to her being allowed to play tennis competitions led to a landmark court case that ultimately gave her the right to play. The controversy became worldwide news. She is a graduate of Yale and the University of Rochester School of Medicine, an Eastern Tennis Hall of Fame inductee, and the author of two books.

For more information,
ninespeakers@usa.net

Find more books from
Keith Publications, LLC
At

www.keithpublications.com

CPSIA information can be obtained at www.ICGtesting.com
Printed in the USA
BVOW03*0156181214

379944BV00003B/5/P